GREEN LANTERN
FEAR ITSELF

RON MARZ
writer

BRAD PARKER
artist

CHRIS ELIOPOULOS
letterer

GREEN LANTERN: FEAR ITSELF. Published by
DC Comics 1700 Broadway, New York, NY 10019.
Copyright © 1999 DC Comics. All Rights Reserved.
All characters featured in this issue, the
distinctive likenesses thereof, and all related
indicia are trademarks of DC Comics. The stories,
characters, and incidents mentioned in this
magazine are entirely fictional. Printed on
recyclable paper.

Printed in Canada.

DC Comics. A division of Warner Bros. -
A Time Warner Entertainment Company

Hard Cover ISBN: 1-56389-310-X
Soft Cover ISBN: 1-56389-311-8

Publication design by KIM GRZYBEK

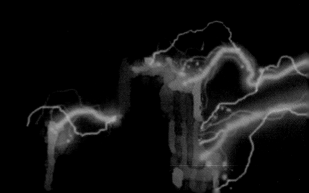

HOW IS IT YOU AMERICANS SAY?
KEEP IT?
HEY, THANKS, BUDDY ...
... YOU HAVE A GOOD DAY NOW, HEAR?
SMITHSONIAN
OH YES ...
... I INTEND TO.

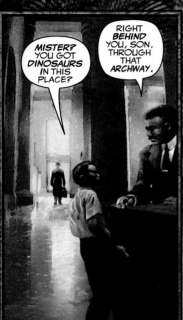

MISTER? YOU GOT DINOSAURS IN THIS PLACE?

RIGHT BEHIND YOU, SON. THROUGH THAT ARCHWAY.

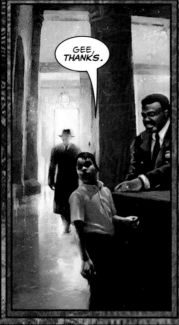

GEE, THANKS.

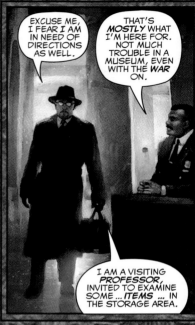

EXCUSE ME, I FEAR I AM IN NEED OF DIRECTIONS AS WELL.

THAT'S MOSTLY WHAT I'M HERE FOR. NOT MUCH TROUBLE IN A MUSEUM, EVEN WITH THE WAR ON.

I AM A VISITING PROFESSOR, INVITED TO EXAMINE SOME ... ITEMS ... IN THE STORAGE AREA.

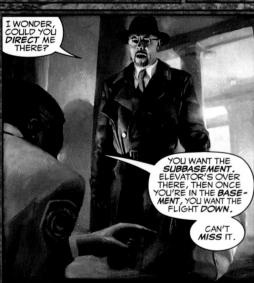

I WONDER, COULD YOU DIRECT ME THERE?

YOU WANT THE SUBBASEMENT. ELEVATOR'S OVER THERE, THEN ONCE YOU'RE IN THE BASEMENT, YOU WANT THE FLIGHT DOWN.

CAN'T MISS IT.

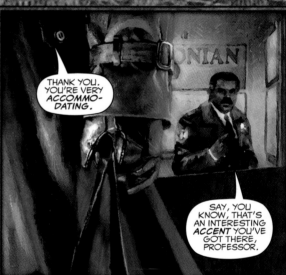

THANK YOU. YOU'RE VERY ACCOMMODATING.

SAY, YOU KNOW, THAT'S AN INTERESTING ACCENT YOU'VE GOT THERE, PROFESSOR.

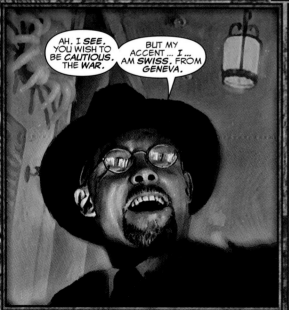

AH. I SEE. YOU WISH TO BE CAUTIOUS. THE WAR.

BUT MY ACCENT ... I ... AM SWISS. FROM GENEVA.

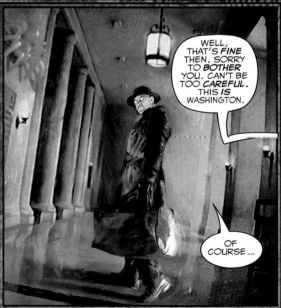

WELL, THAT'S FINE THEN. SORRY TO BOTHER YOU. CAN'T BE TOO CAREFUL. THIS IS WASHINGTON.

OF COURSE ...

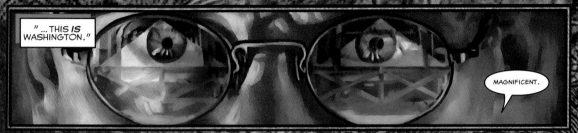

"...THIS *IS* WASHINGTON."

MAGNIFICENT.

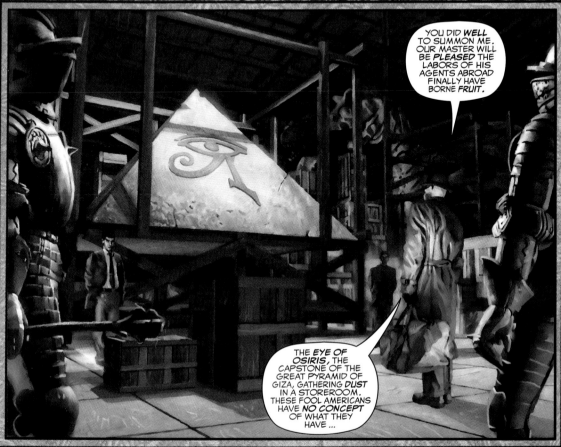

YOU DID *WELL* TO SUMMON ME. OUR MASTER WILL BE *PLEASED* THE LABORS OF HIS AGENTS ABROAD FINALLY HAVE BORNE *FRUIT*.

THE *EYE OF OSIRIS,* THE CAPSTONE OF THE GREAT PYRAMID OF GIZA, GATHERING *DUST* IN A STOREROOM. THESE FOOL AMERICANS HAVE *NO CONCEPT* OF WHAT THEY HAVE ...

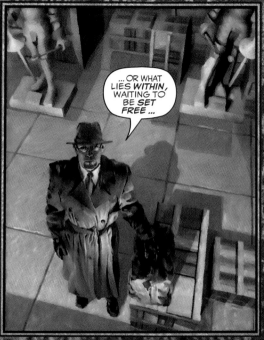

... OR WHAT LIES *WITHIN,* WAITING TO BE *SET FREE* ...

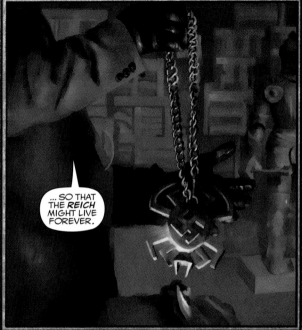

... SO THAT THE *REICH* MIGHT LIVE FOREVER.

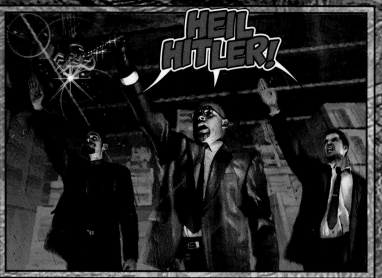

HEIL HITLER!

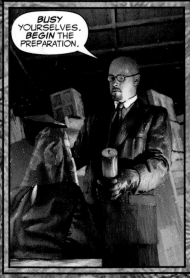

BUSY YOURSELVES. *BEGIN* THE PREPARATION.

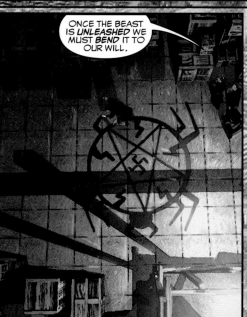

ONCE THE BEAST IS *UNLEASHED* WE MUST *BEND* IT TO OUR WILL.

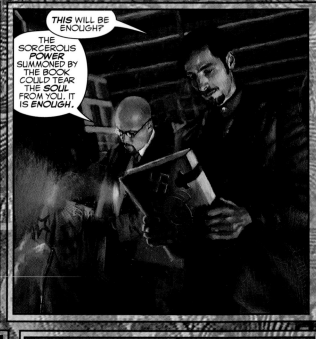

THIS WILL BE ENOUGH?

THE SORCEROUS *POWER* SUMMONED BY THE BOOK COULD TEAR THE *SOUL* FROM YOU. IT IS *ENOUGH*.

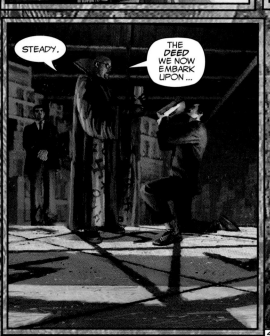

STEADY.

THE *DEED* WE NOW EMBARK UPON ...

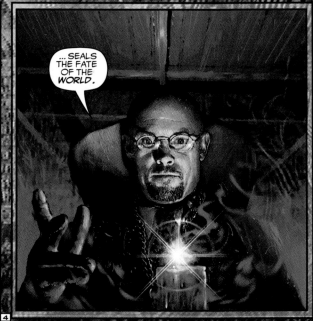

... SEALS THE FATE OF THE *WORLD*.

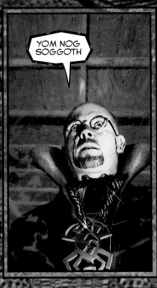

YOM NOG SOGGOTH

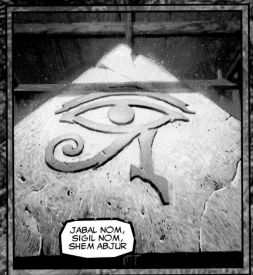

JABAL NOM, SIGIL NOM, SHEM ABJUR

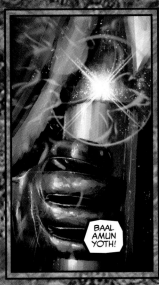

BAAL AMUN YOTH!

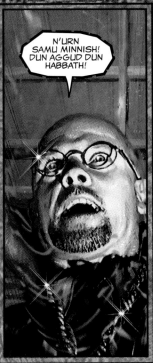

N'URN SAMU MINNISH! DUN AGGUD DUN HABBATH!

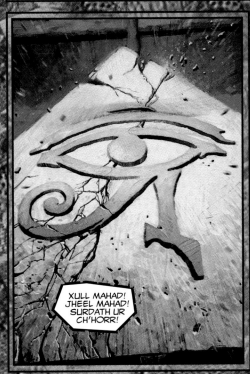

XULL MAHAD! JHEEL MAHAD! SURDATH UR CH'HORR!

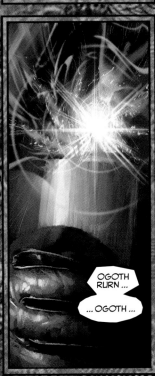

OGOTH RURN ...

... OGOTH ...

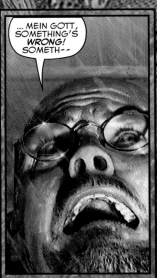

... MEIN GOTT, SOMETHING'S *WRONG!* SOMETH--

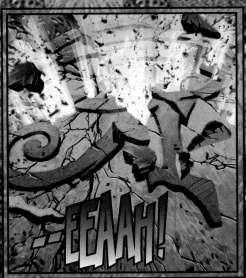

--EEAAH!

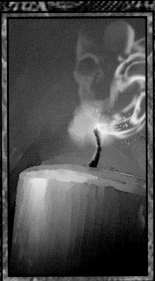

ANY CHANCE OF A FEW MORE *SMILES?*
NO, I DIDN'T *THINK* SO. ALL RIGHT THEN, EVERYONE *HOLD* FOR JUST ONE MORE ...
... AND WE'RE *DONE*.
FAASH
ALLOW *ME*, MR. PRESIDENT.
THANK YOU, GREEN LANTERN. AND THANK YOU FOR *COMING*, YOU AND THE OTHERS.

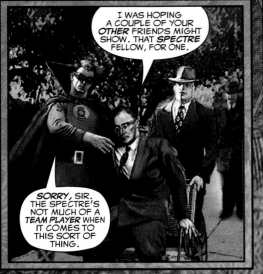

I WAS HOPING A COUPLE OF YOUR *OTHER* FRIENDS MIGHT SHOW. THAT *SPECTRE* FELLOW, FOR ONE.

SORRY, SIR. THE SPECTRE'S NOT MUCH OF A *TEAM PLAYER* WHEN IT COMES TO THIS SORT OF THING.

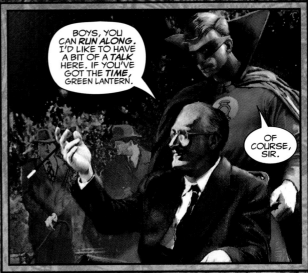

BOYS, YOU CAN *RUN ALONG.* I'D LIKE TO HAVE A BIT OF A *TALK* HERE. IF YOU'VE GOT THE *TIME,* GREEN LANTERN.

OF COURSE, SIR.

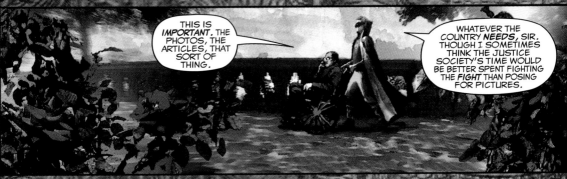

THIS IS *IMPORTANT.* THE PHOTOS, THE ARTICLES, THAT SORT OF THING.

WHATEVER THE COUNTRY *NEEDS,* SIR. THOUGH I SOMETIMES THINK THE JUSTICE SOCIETY'S TIME WOULD BE BETTER SPENT FIGHTING THE *FIGHT* THAN POSING FOR PICTURES.

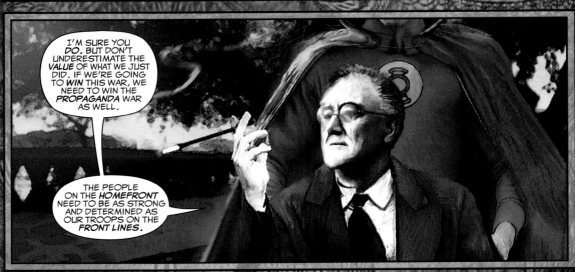

I'M SURE YOU *DO.* BUT DON'T UNDERESTIMATE THE *VALUE* OF WHAT WE JUST DID. IF WE'RE GOING TO *WIN* THIS WAR, WE NEED TO WIN THE *PROPAGANDA* WAR AS WELL.

THE PEOPLE ON THE *HOMEFRONT* NEED TO BE AS STRONG AND DETERMINED AS OUR TROOPS ON THE *FRONT LINES.*

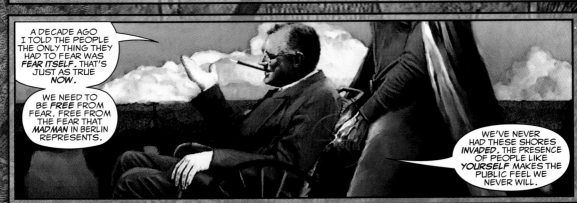

A DECADE AGO I TOLD THE PEOPLE THE ONLY THING THEY HAD TO FEAR WAS *FEAR ITSELF.* THAT'S JUST AS TRUE *NOW.*

WE NEED TO BE *FREE* FROM FEAR. FREE FROM THE FEAR THAT *MADMAN* IN BERLIN REPRESENTS.

WE'VE NEVER HAD THESE SHORES *INVADED.* THE PRESENCE OF PEOPLE LIKE *YOURSELF* MAKES THE PUBLIC FEEL WE NEVER WILL.

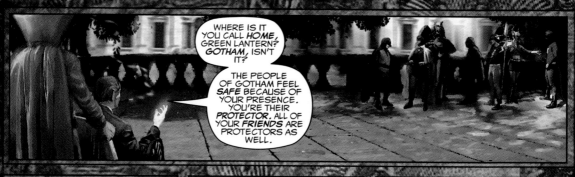

WHERE IS IT YOU CALL *HOME*, GREEN LANTERN? *GOTHAM*, ISN'T IT?

THE PEOPLE OF GOTHAM FEEL *SAFE* BECAUSE OF YOUR PRESENCE. YOU'RE THEIR *PROTECTOR*. ALL OF YOUR *FRIENDS* ARE PROTECTORS AS WELL.

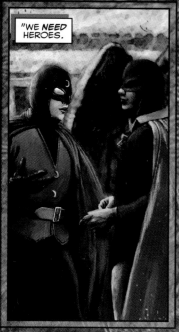

"WE *NEED* HEROES.

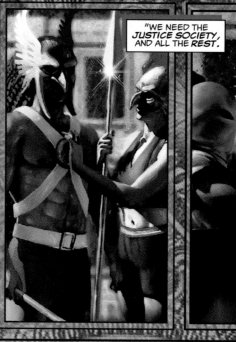

"WE NEED THE *JUSTICE SOCIETY*, AND ALL THE *REST*.

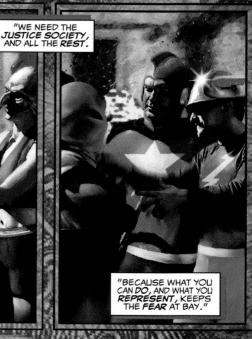

"BECAUSE WHAT YOU CAN *DO*, AND WHAT YOU *REPRESENT*, KEEPS THE *FEAR* AT BAY."

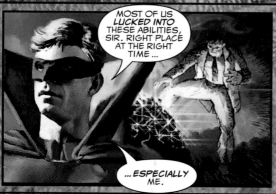

MOST OF US *LUCKED INTO* THESE ABILITIES, SIR. RIGHT PLACE AT THE RIGHT TIME ...

...ESPECIALLY ME.

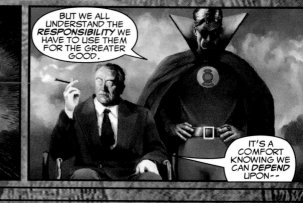

BUT WE ALL UNDERSTAND THE *RESPONSIBILITY* WE HAVE TO USE THEM FOR THE GREATER GOOD.

IT'S A COMFORT KNOWING WE CAN *DEPEND* UPON--

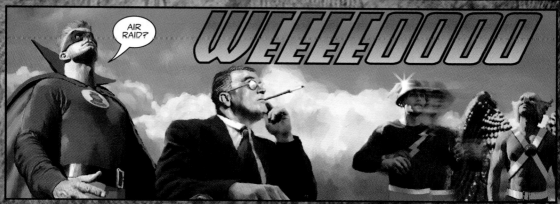

AIR RAID?

WEEEEOOOO

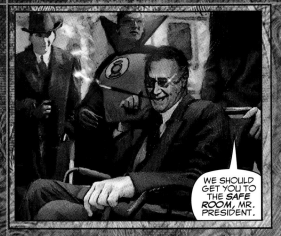

WE SHOULD GET YOU TO THE *SAFE ROOM*, MR. PRESIDENT.

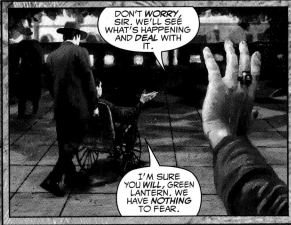

DON'T *WORRY*, SIR. WE'LL SEE WHAT'S HAPPENING AND *DEAL* WITH IT.

I'M SURE YOU *WILL*, GREEN LANTERN. WE HAVE *NOTHING* TO FEAR.

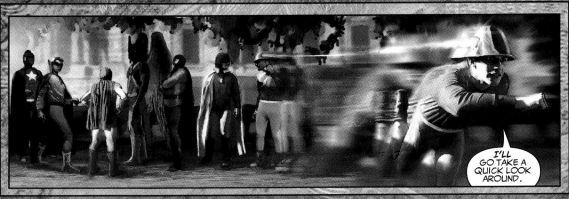

I'LL GO TAKE A QUICK LOOK AROUND.

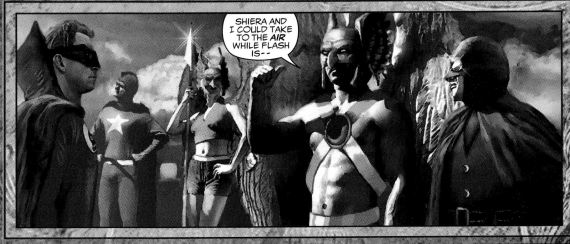

SHIERA AND I COULD TAKE TO THE *AIR* WHILE FLASH IS--

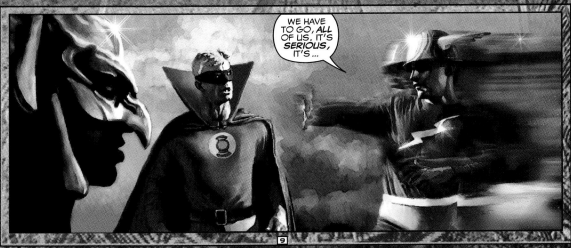

WE HAVE TO GO, *ALL* OF US. IT'S *SERIOUS*, IT'S ...

9

"...WELL, I DON'T EXACTLY KNOW WHAT IT IS."

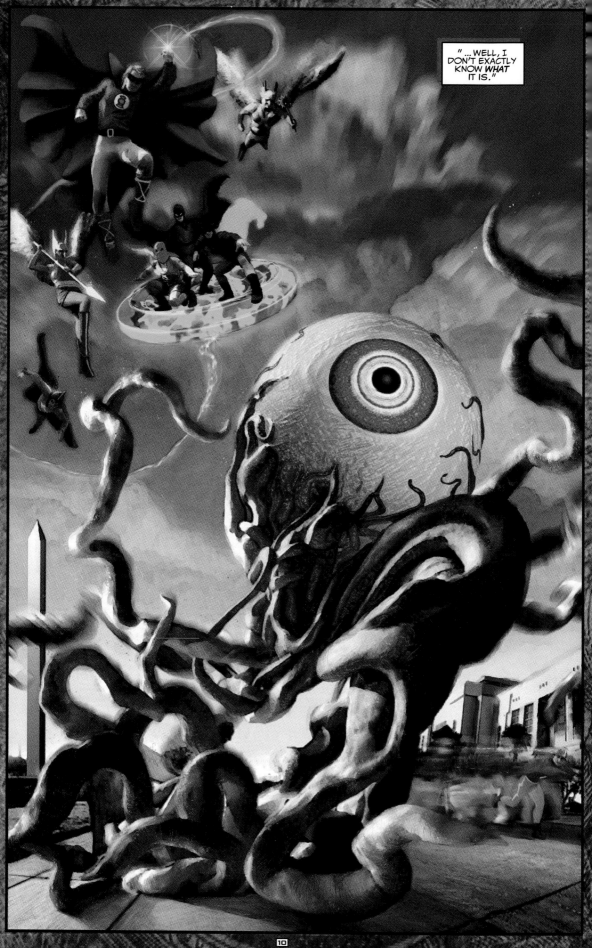

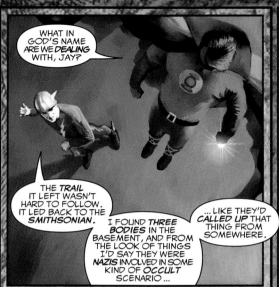

WHAT IN GOD'S NAME ARE WE *DEALING* WITH, JAY?

THE *TRAIL* IT LEFT WASN'T HARD TO FOLLOW. IT LED BACK TO THE *SMITHSONIAN*.

I FOUND *THREE BODIES* IN THE BASEMENT, AND FROM THE LOOK OF THINGS I'D SAY THEY WERE *NAZIS* INVOLVED IN SOME KIND OF *OCCULT* SCENARIO ...

... LIKE THEY'D *CALLED UP* THAT THING FROM SOMEWHERE.

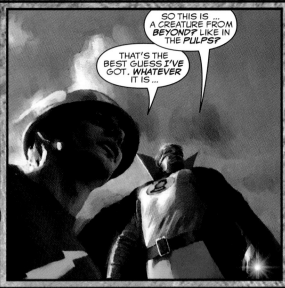

SO THIS IS ... A *CREATURE FROM BEYOND?* LIKE IN THE *PULPS?*

THAT'S THE BEST GUESS I'VE GOT. *WHATEVER* IT IS ...

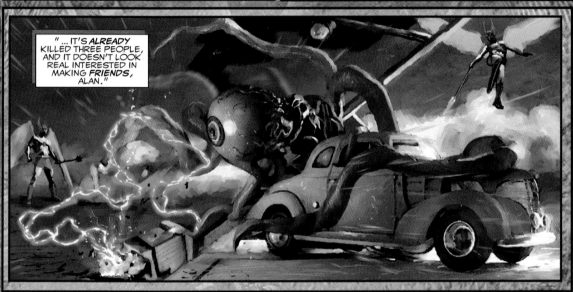

" ... IT'S *ALREADY* KILLED THREE PEOPLE, AND IT DOESN'T LOOK REAL INTERESTED IN MAKING *FRIENDS,* ALAN."

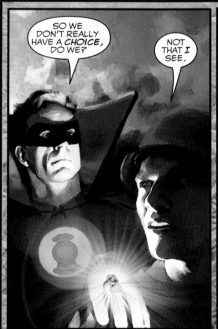

SO WE DON'T REALLY HAVE A *CHOICE,* DO WE?

NOT THAT *I* SEE.

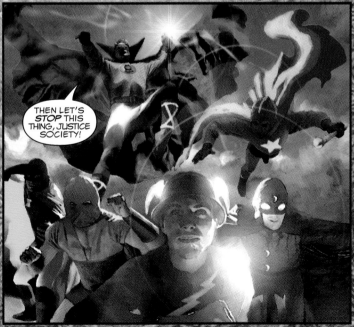

THEN LET'S *STOP* THIS THING, JUSTICE SOCIETY!

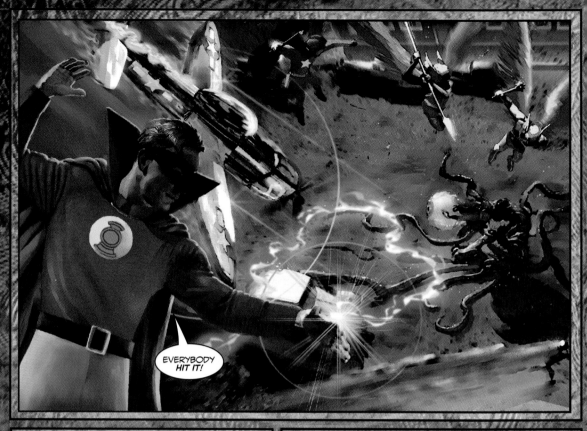

EVERYBODY HIT IT!

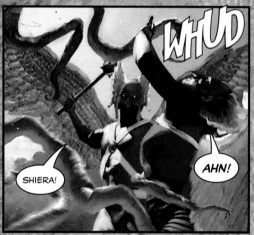

SHIERA!

AHN!

WHUD

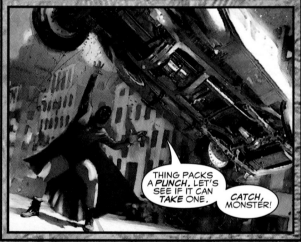

THING PACKS A *PUNCH.* LET'S SEE IF IT CAN *TAKE* ONE.

CATCH, MONSTER!

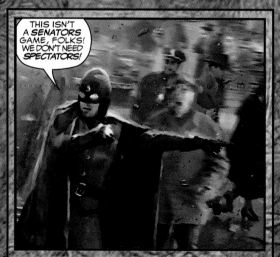

THIS ISN'T A *SENATORS* GAME, FOLKS! WE DON'T NEED *SPECTATORS!*

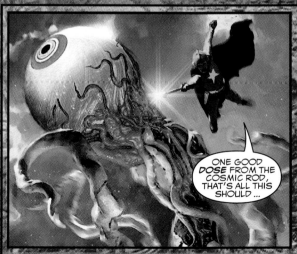

ONE GOOD *DOSE* FROM THE COSMIC ROD, THAT'S ALL THIS SHOULD ...

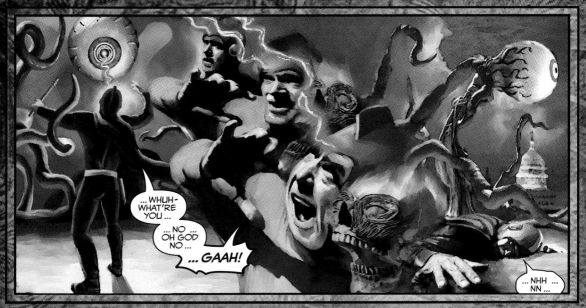

... WHUH-
WHAT'RE
YOU ...

... NO ...
OH GOD
NO ...

... GAAH!

... NHH ...
NN ...

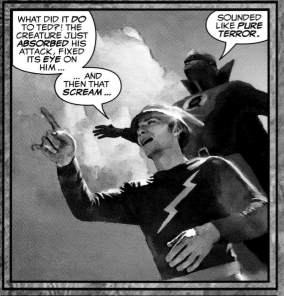

WHAT DID IT DO
TO TED?! THE
CREATURE JUST
ABSORBED HIS
ATTACK, FIXED
ITS EYE ON
HIM ...

SOUNDED
LIKE PURE
TERROR.

... AND
THEN THAT
SCREAM ...

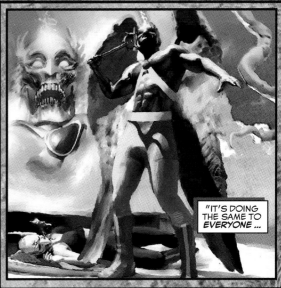

"IT'S DOING
THE SAME TO
EVERYONE ...

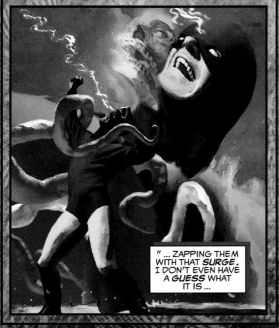

" ... ZAPPING THEM
WITH THAT SURGE.
I DON'T EVEN HAVE
A GUESS WHAT
IT IS ...

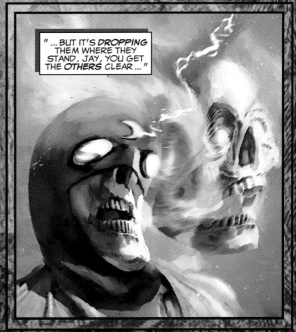

" ... BUT IT'S DROPPING
THEM WHERE THEY
STAND. JAY, YOU GET
THE OTHERS CLEAR ... "

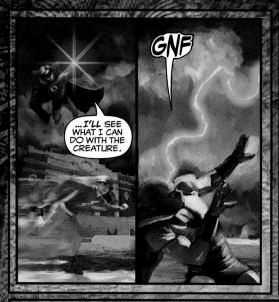

...I'LL SEE WHAT I CAN DO WITH THE CREATURE.

GNF

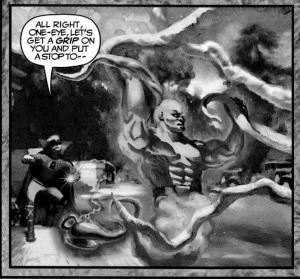

ALL RIGHT, ONE-EYE, LET'S GET A *GRIP* ON YOU AND PUT A STOP TO--

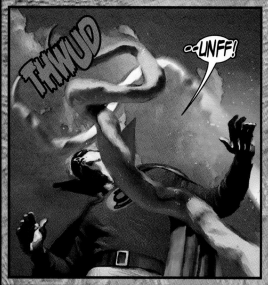

THWUD

--UNFF!

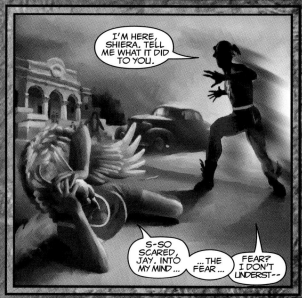

I'M HERE, SHIERA. TELL ME WHAT IT DID TO YOU.

S-SO SCARED, JAY. INTO MY MIND ...

... THE FEAR ...

FEAR? I DON'T UNDERST--

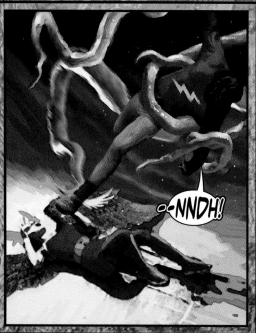

--NNDH!

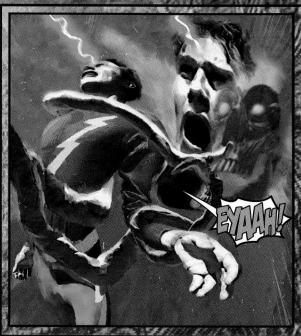

EYAAH!

14

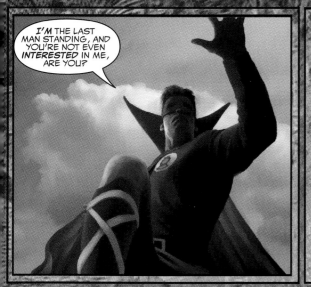

I'M THE LAST MAN STANDING, AND YOU'RE NOT EVEN *INTERESTED* IN ME, ARE YOU?

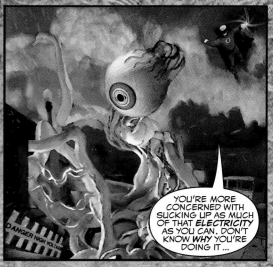

YOU'RE MORE CONCERNED WITH SUCKING UP AS MUCH OF THAT *ELECTRICITY* AS YOU CAN. DON'T KNOW *WHY* YOU'RE DOING IT ...

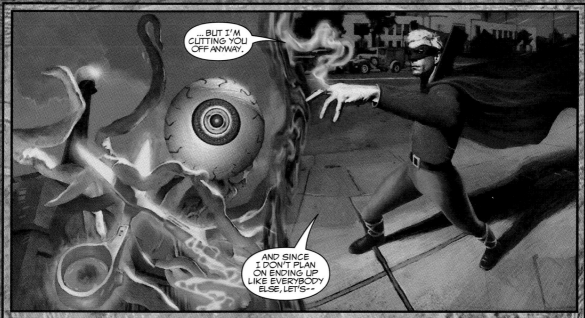

... BUT I'M *CUTTING YOU OFF ANYWAY.*

AND SINCE I DON'T PLAN ON ENDING UP LIKE EVERYBODY ELSE, LET'S--

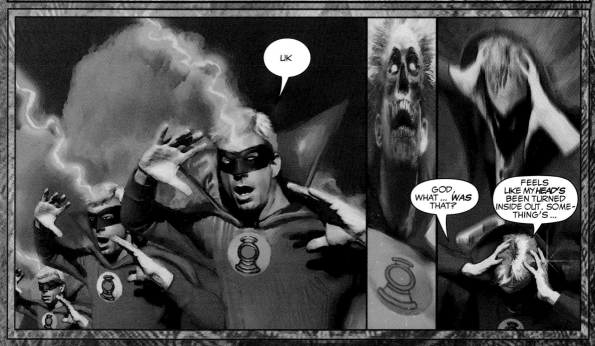

UK

GOD, WHAT ... *WAS* THAT?

FEELS LIKE MY *HEAD'S* BEEN TURNED INSIDE OUT. SOME-THING'S ...

...WRONG.
IT ... IT CAN'T BE. THIS IS SOME KIND OF NIGHTMARE.
NIGHTMARE? YOU'RE RIGHT, ALAN ...

...YOU SHOULD BE AFRAID.

JAY? WHAT'S--
--UNF!
WHY ARE YOU FIGHTING IT! WE DIDN'T! WE COULDN'T!

GIVE IN TO YOUR FEAR, ALAN!

NO...
...THIS CAN'T BE REAL...

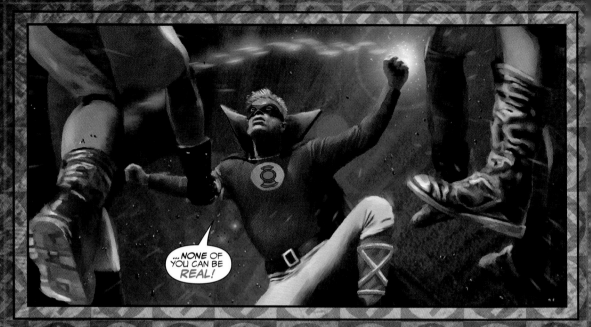

...NONE OF YOU CAN BE REAL!

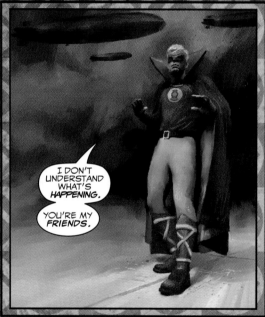

I DON'T UNDERSTAND WHAT'S HAPPENING.

YOU'RE MY FRIENDS.

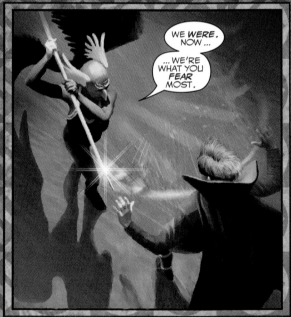

WE WERE. NOW...

...WE'RE WHAT YOU FEAR MOST.

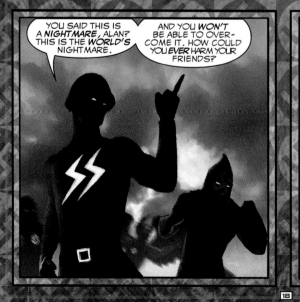

YOU SAID THIS IS A NIGHTMARE, ALAN? THIS IS THE WORLD'S NIGHTMARE.

AND YOU WON'T BE ABLE TO OVER-COME IT. HOW COULD YOU EVER HARM YOUR FRIENDS?

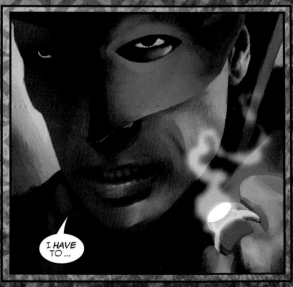

I HAVE TO...

... BECAUSE GOD FORGIVE ME, THERE'S NO OTHER CHOICE.
ALAN, PLEASE ...
... DON'T DO THIS TO US ...
I'M SORRY, JAY. I'M SO ...

...YOU!
IT'S NOT THEM! IT NEVER WAS!
IT'S YOU!
YOU DIGGING INTO MY HEAD AND PLAYING OUT MY FEARS LIKE A NEWSREEL!
I AM AFRAID OF WHAT MIGHT HAPPEN IF WE LOSE THE WAR, AFRAID THE WHOLE WORLD WILL BE CORRUPTED! BUT THAT DOESN'T MEAN I GIVE IN TO IT!
I HAD THE WILLPOWER TO BURN AWAY MY FEARS ...
...I'LL DO THE SAME TO YOU!

"HEY ..."

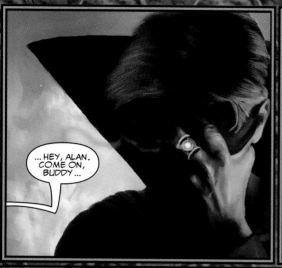

...HEY, ALAN. COME ON, BUDDY...

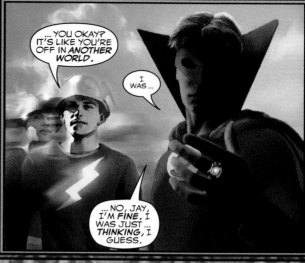

...YOU OKAY? IT'S LIKE YOU'RE OFF IN *ANOTHER WORLD*.

I WAS...

...NO, JAY. I'M *FINE*. I WAS JUST... *THINKING*, I GUESS.

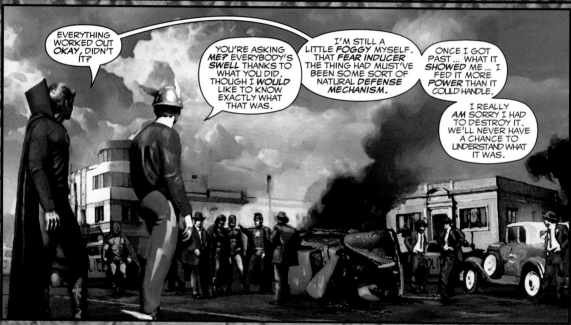

EVERYTHING WORKED OUT *OKAY*, DIDN'T IT?

YOU'RE ASKING *ME*? EVERYBODY'S *SWELL* THANKS TO WHAT YOU DID. THOUGH I *WOULD* LIKE TO KNOW EXACTLY WHAT THAT WAS.

I'M STILL A LITTLE *FOGGY* MYSELF. THAT *FEAR INDUCER* THE THING HAD MUST'VE BEEN SOME SORT OF NATURAL *DEFENSE MECHANISM*.

ONCE I GOT PAST... WHAT IT *SHOWED* ME... I FED IT MORE *POWER* THAN IT COULD HANDLE.

I REALLY *AM* SORRY I HAD TO DESTROY IT. WE'LL NEVER HAVE A CHANCE TO UNDERSTAND WHAT IT WAS.

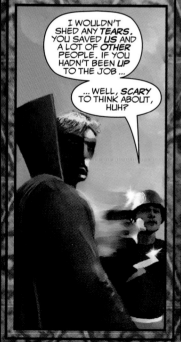

I WOULDN'T SHED ANY *TEARS*. YOU SAVED *US* AND A LOT OF *OTHER* PEOPLE. IF YOU HADN'T BEEN *UP* TO THE JOB...

...WELL, *SCARY* TO THINK ABOUT, HUH?

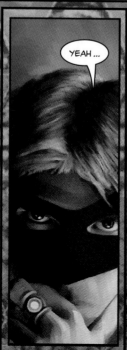

YEAH...

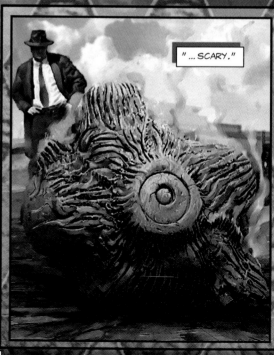

"...SCARY."

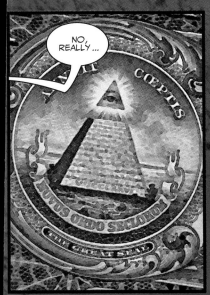

NO, REALLY ...

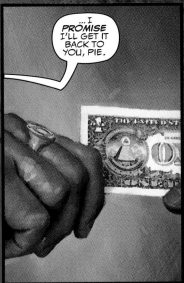

... I PROMISE I'LL GET IT BACK TO YOU, PIE.

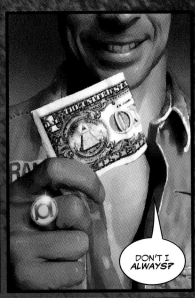

DON'T I ALWAYS?

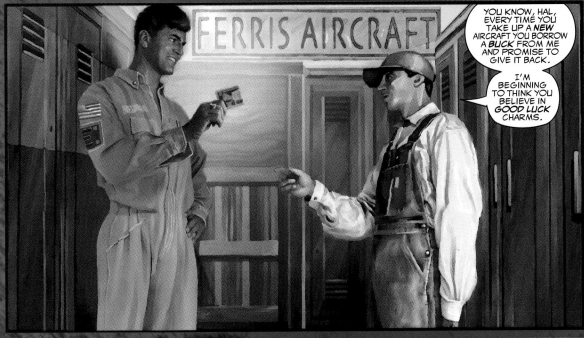

YOU KNOW, HAL, EVERY TIME YOU TAKE UP A NEW AIRCRAFT YOU BORROW A BUCK FROM ME AND PROMISE TO GIVE IT BACK.

I'M BEGINNING TO THINK YOU BELIEVE IN GOOD LUCK CHARMS.

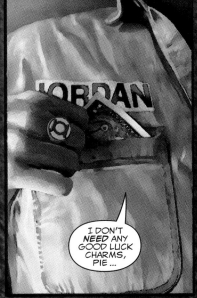

I DON'T NEED ANY GOOD LUCK CHARMS, PIE ...

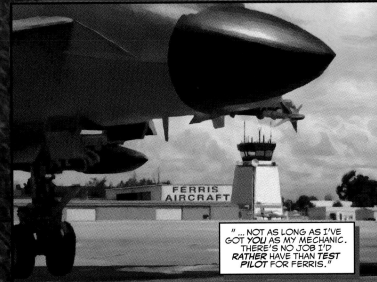

" ... NOT AS LONG AS I'VE GOT YOU AS MY MECHANIC. THERE'S NO JOB I'D RATHER HAVE THAN TEST PILOT FOR FERRIS."

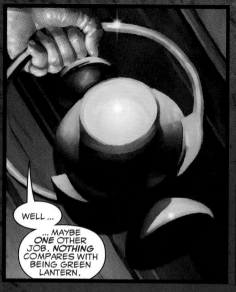

WELL ...

... MAYBE ONE OTHER JOB. *NOTHING* COMPARES WITH BEING GREEN LANTERN.

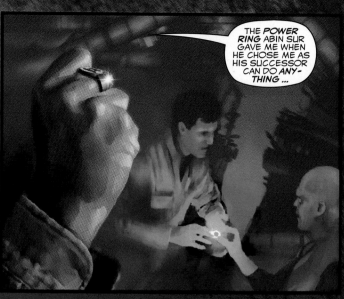

THE *POWER RING* ABIN SUR GAVE ME WHEN HE CHOSE ME AS HIS SUCCESSOR CAN DO *ANY-THING* ...

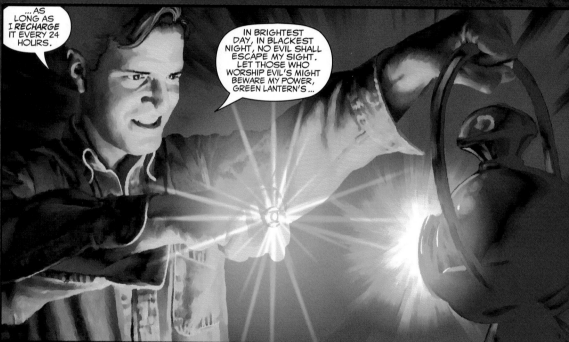

...AS LONG AS I *RECHARGE* IT EVERY 24 HOURS.

IN BRIGHTEST DAY, IN BLACKEST NIGHT, NO EVIL SHALL ESCAPE MY SIGHT. LET THOSE WHO WORSHIP EVIL'S MIGHT BEWARE MY POWER, GREEN LANTERN'S ...

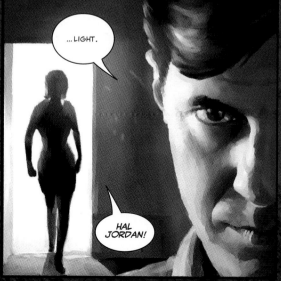

...LIGHT.

HAL JORDAN!

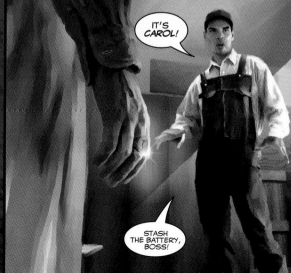

IT'S CAROL!

STASH THE BATTERY, BOSS!

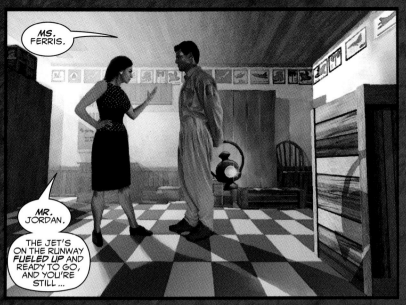

MS. FERRIS.

MR. JORDAN. THE JET'S ON THE RUNWAY *FUELED UP* AND READY TO GO, AND YOU'RE STILL ...

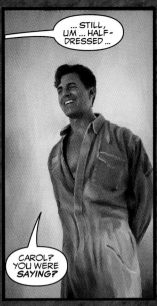

... STILL, UM ... HALF-DRESSED ...

CAROL? YOU WERE *SAYING?*

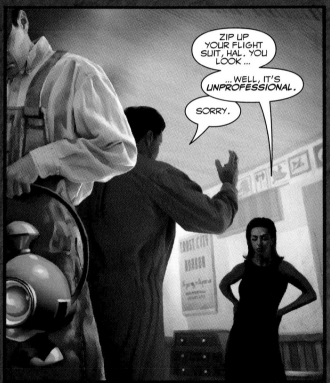

ZIP UP YOUR FLIGHT SUIT, HAL. YOU LOOK ...

... WELL, IT'S *UNPROFESSIONAL.*

SORRY.

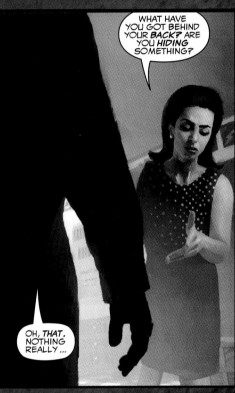

WHAT HAVE YOU GOT BEHIND YOUR *BACK?* ARE YOU *HIDING* SOMETHING?

OH, *THAT.* NOTHING REALLY ...

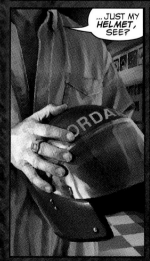

... JUST MY *HELMET,* SEE?

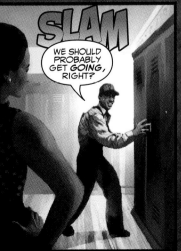

SLAM

WE SHOULD PROBABLY GET *GOING,* RIGHT?

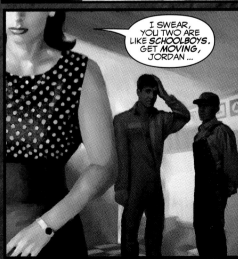

I SWEAR, YOU TWO ARE LIKE *SCHOOLBOYS.* GET *MOVING,* JORDAN ...

"... AND GET YOUR BUTT INTO THAT COCKPIT."
I'VE GONE OVER THIS BIRD THREE TIMES AND EVERYTHING CHECKS OUT, BOSS. SHOULD BE A SMOOTH RIDE ...
... AS LONG AS YOU TAKE IT EASY. FIRST TIME UP WE JUST WANT YOU TO RUN THE BASICS AND THEN SET HER DOWN.
PIE, I'M A TEST PILOT, NOT A LITTLE OLD LADY.
IT'S MY JOB TO GIVE THESE PLANES A SHAKEDOWN. WE DON'T WANT THE RUSSIANS GETTING TOO FAR AHEAD OF US IN THE HARDWARE DEPARTMENT, RIGHT?
ALL I'M SAYING IS BRING IT BACK IN ONE PIECE. AND YOU WITH IT.
THAT DOLLAR'S ONLY A LOAN.
REMEMBER, FEARLESS, NO HOT-DOGGING!
COME ON, PIE...
"... LET'S NOT FORGET WHO YOU'RE TALKING TO."
SHREEEEEEE
OH, THAT MAN!

SHE FEELS **GOOD**. HANDLES **GREAT**, NICE AND RESPONSIVE.
WISH I KNEW MORE **WOMEN** LIKE THAT.
HAL.
IT'S **CAROL** ON THE OTHER END.
OOPS.
WE'RE ONLY RUNNING THE **PRELIMINARY** CHECKLIST. WE **DON'T** WANT YOU PUTTING THE PLANE THROUGH ITS PACES YET.
SURE, I UNDERSTAND. NO **DAREDEVIL** STUFF.
HANG ON, WHAT IS **THAT?**
HAL? SAY **AGAIN** PLEASE?

I SEE SOMETHING DOWN IN THE WATER.
YOU'RE OUT OVER THE WATER?! THE FLIGHT PLAN DIDN'T CALL FOR YOU TO BE--
I THINK ... BOY, YOU'RE NOT GONNA BELIEVE THIS. IT'S A SUB.
HAL, DID YOU SAY A SUB? A SUBMARINE?
YES, NOT A HUGE ONE, ONE OF THOSE MINI JOBS, ENOUGH FOR MAYBE TWO PEOPLE.
WHY WOULD A SUB BE ...
... UH-OH.
I'VE GOT A PROBLEM HERE.
WHAT KIND OF PROBLEM?
A MISSILE KIND OF PROBLEM.
HAL, ARE YOU SAYING THE SUB FIRED ON YOU?
HAL?

"HAL?!"

BCHOOM!

OH MY GOD ...

CAROL'S GONNA KILL ME ...
... UNLESS I COME UP WITH A PRETTY GOOD EXPLANATION OF WHY HER FATHER'S MULTI-MILLION-DOLLAR PROTOTYPE IS RAINING DOWN ALL OVER THE PACIFIC RIGHT NOW.
... AND HOW I CAME THROUGH UNSCATHED.
ЭТО АМЕРИАНСКИЙ ГЕРОЙ! УЕИВАЙТЕ ЕГО!
SO ...
... I'M GUESSING YOU GUYS AREN'T FROM AROUND HERE.
BRAAP BRAAP BRAAP
BCHOW BCHOW

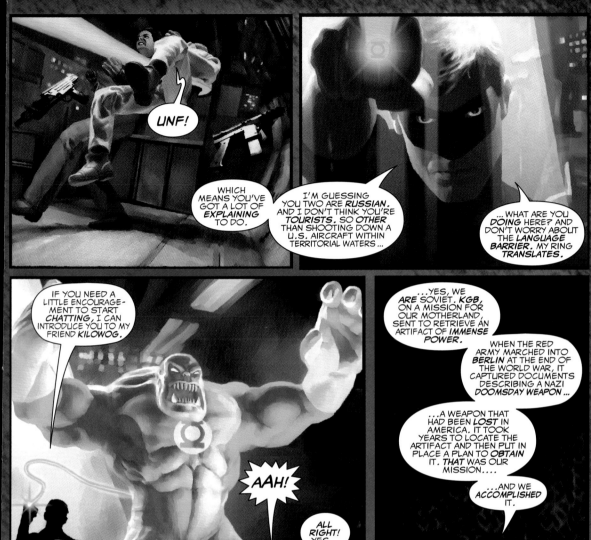

UNF!

WHICH MEANS YOU'VE GOT A LOT OF *EXPLAINING* TO DO.

I'M GUESSING YOU TWO ARE *RUSSIAN*. AND I DON'T THINK YOU'RE *TOURISTS*. SO *OTHER* THAN SHOOTING DOWN A U.S. AIRCRAFT WITHIN TERRITORIAL WATERS ...

... WHAT ARE YOU *DOING* HERE? AND DON'T WORRY ABOUT THE *LANGUAGE BARRIER*. MY RING *TRANSLATES*.

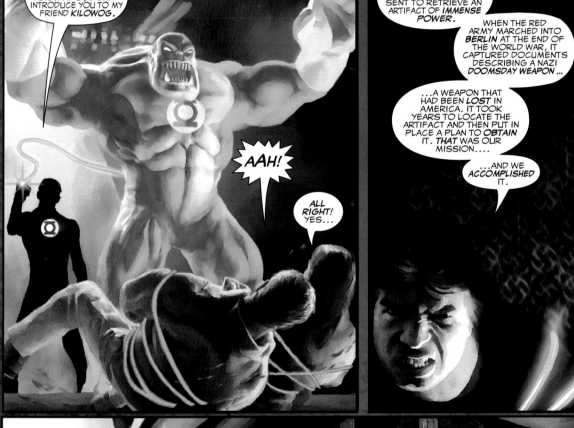

IF YOU NEED A LITTLE ENCOURAGE-MENT TO START *CHATTING*, I CAN INTRODUCE YOU TO MY FRIEND *KILOWOG*.

AAH!

ALL RIGHT! YES...

...YES, WE *ARE* SOVIET. *KGB*, ON A MISSION FOR OUR MOTHERLAND, SENT TO RETRIEVE AN ARTIFACT OF *IMMENSE POWER*.

WHEN THE RED ARMY MARCHED INTO *BERLIN* AT THE END OF THE WORLD WAR, IT CAPTURED DOCUMENTS DESCRIBING A NAZI *DOOMSDAY WEAPON* ...

...A WEAPON THAT HAD BEEN *LOST* IN AMERICA. IT TOOK YEARS TO LOCATE THE ARTIFACT AND THEN PUT IN PLACE A PLAN TO *OBTAIN* IT. *THAT* WAS OUR MISSION....

...AND WE *ACCOMPLISHED* IT.

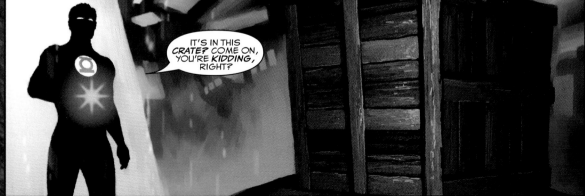

IT'S IN THIS *CRATE?* COME ON, YOU'RE *KIDDING*, RIGHT?

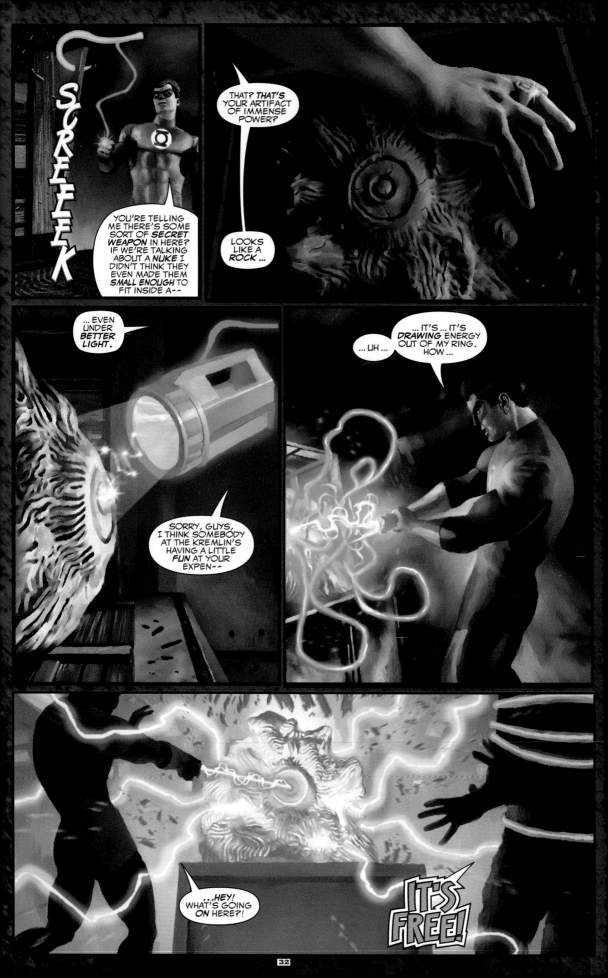

SCREEEK

THAT? *THAT'S* YOUR *ARTIFACT OF IMMENSE POWER?*

YOU'RE TELLING ME THERE'S SOME SORT OF *SECRET WEAPON* IN HERE? IF WE'RE TALKING ABOUT A *NUKE* I DIDN'T THINK THEY EVEN MADE THEM *SMALL ENOUGH* TO FIT INSIDE A--

LOOKS LIKE A *ROCK*...

... EVEN UNDER *BETTER LIGHT.*

SORRY, GUYS, I THINK SOMEBODY AT THE KREMLIN'S HAVING A LITTLE *FUN* AT YOUR EXPEN--

... IT'S... IT'S *DRAWING* ENERGY OUT OF MY RING. HOW...

... UH...

...HEY! WHAT'S GOING ON HERE?!

IT'S FREE!

WHAT'S FREE?
THOUGH I SUPPOSE WE'RE ABOUT TO FIND OUT.
KRACHOOM
UNDER OTHER CIRCUMSTANCES I'D BE HAULING YOU OFF TO JAIL, BUT WE'VE BOTH GOT JOBS TO DO.
I WANT YOU TWO TO GO TO THE HARBOR MASTER, TELL HIM TO EVACUATE THE AREA...
... WHILE I DEAL WITH WHATEVER'S GOING ON OUT THERE.
COAST CITY HARBOR

OH BOY.

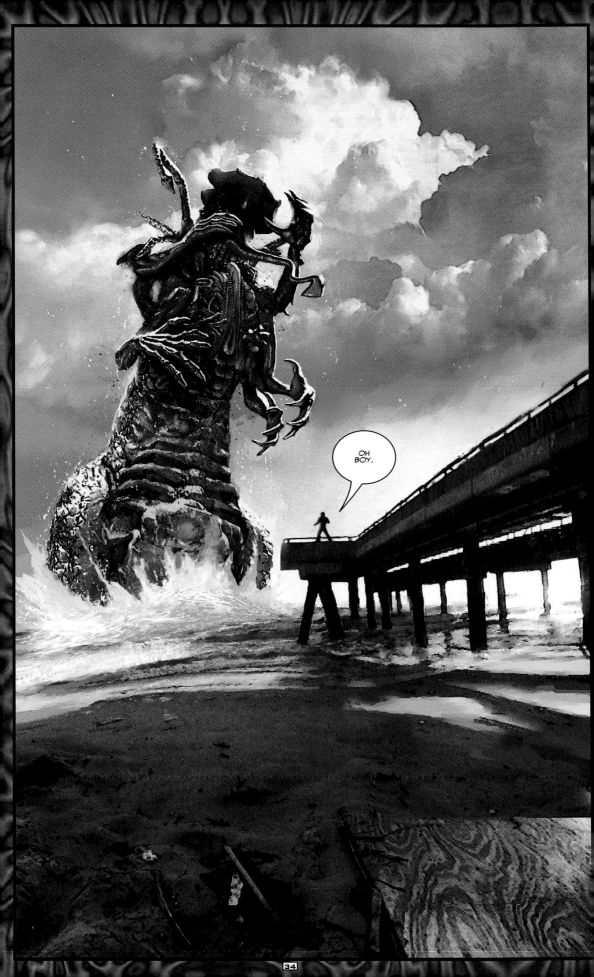

WELL ...
... AT LEAST IT'S NOT YELLOW.
MEANING I SHOULD BE ABLE TO HOLD IT BACK ...
... OR NOT.
THING'S ABSORBING THE RING ENERGY AGAIN, JUST LIKE--
THWUD
WHFF!

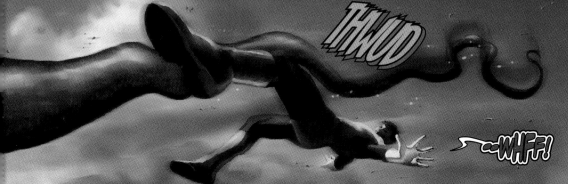

GREEN LANTERN!
GHN!
MISTER ...
...RUN!
I MIGHT NOT BE UP TO HANDLING THIS ONE. NOT ALONE, ANYWAY.
THIS IS GREEN LANTERN ON THE JLA COMMUNICATOR FREQUENCY. I HOPE SOMEBODY'S LISTENING ...
BEEP
... BECAUSE I COULD USE A LITTLE HELP IN COAST CITY. IF YOU'RE GETTING THIS, COME RUNNING.
AND HURRY.

STEADY ...

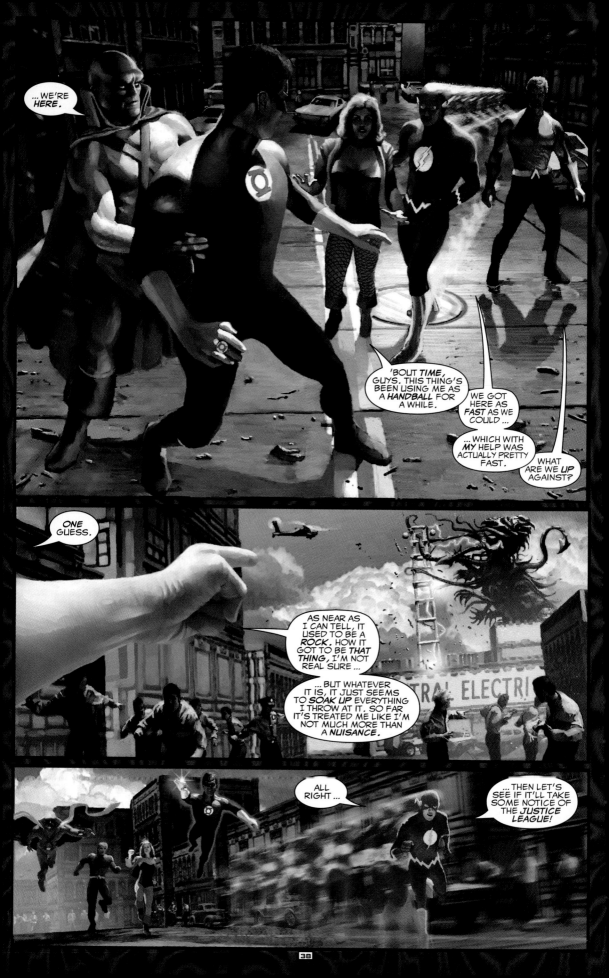

...WE'RE HERE.

'BOUT TIME, GUYS. THIS THING'S BEEN USING ME AS A HANDBALL FOR A WHILE.

WE GOT HERE AS FAST AS WE COULD...

...WHICH WITH MY HELP WAS ACTUALLY PRETTY FAST.

WHAT ARE WE UP AGAINST?

ONE GUESS.

AS NEAR AS I CAN TELL, IT USED TO BE A ROCK. HOW IT GOT TO BE THAT THING, I'M NOT REAL SURE...

...BUT WHATEVER IT IS, IT JUST SEEMS TO SOAK UP EVERYTHING I THROW AT IT. SO FAR IT'S TREATED ME LIKE I'M NOT MUCH MORE THAN A NUISANCE.

CENTRAL ELECTRI

ALL RIGHT...

...THEN LET'S SEE IF IT'LL TAKE SOME NOTICE OF THE JUSTICE LEAGUE!

VVVVMMM
THAKK
KRUNK
EEEEEEEEEEEEE
AT LEAST IT'S *LOOKING* AT US NOW.

UM ...
... YOU SURE THAT'S SUCH A GREAT IDEA?
HAL, WHAT'S IT DOING, TURNING THAT EYE ON ALL OF--
AAGH!
GAAH ...
... GHH ...
... NHH ...
... WHAT ...
... WHAT WAS THAT? BARRY?

MY GOD.
NUCLEAR HOLOCAUST IN COAST CITY. BUT WHAT COULD'VE CAUSED ... WAS IT THE CREATURE? OR A RUSSIAN ATTACK? I DON'T ...
... OH NO. ARTHUR.
DINAH ...
... AND BARRY ...
... FIRE ...
... AND J'ONN?

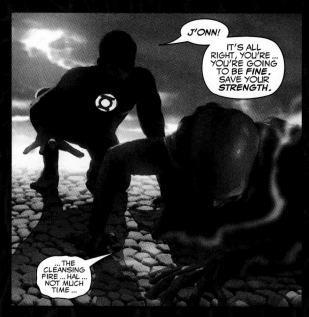

J'ONN! IT'S ALL RIGHT, YOU'RE... YOU'RE GOING TO BE *FINE.* SAVE YOUR *STRENGTH.*

...THE CLEANSING FIRE... HAL... NOT MUCH TIME...

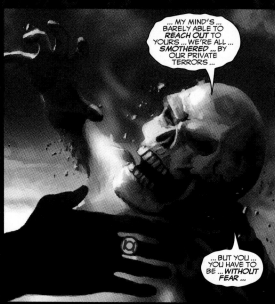

...MY MIND'S... BARELY ABLE TO *REACH OUT* TO YOURS... WE'RE ALL... *SMOTHERED*... BY OUR PRIVATE TERRORS...

...BUT YOU... YOU HAVE TO BE... *WITHOUT FEAR*...

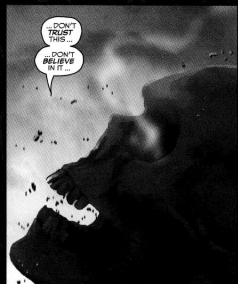

...DON'T *TRUST* THIS... ...DON'T *BELIEVE* IN IT...

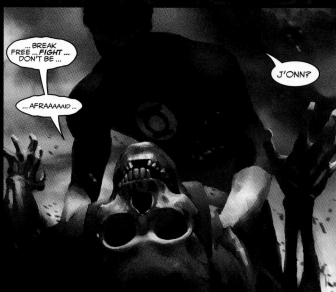

...BREAK FREE... *FIGHT*... DON'T BE...

...AFRAAAAAID...

J'ONN?

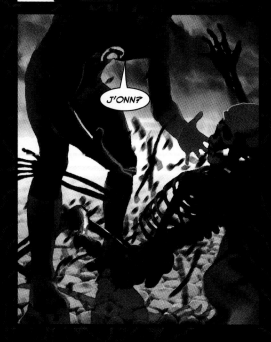

J'ONN?

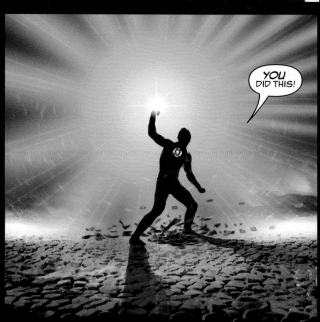

YOU DID THIS!

42

BUT YOU'RE NOT GOING TO TRAP ME INSIDE A NIGHTMARE!
THIS IS MY CITY!
I WILL PROTECT IT!
AND YOU'RE NOT ...
... GOING TO SCARE ME OFF!

"HAL?"

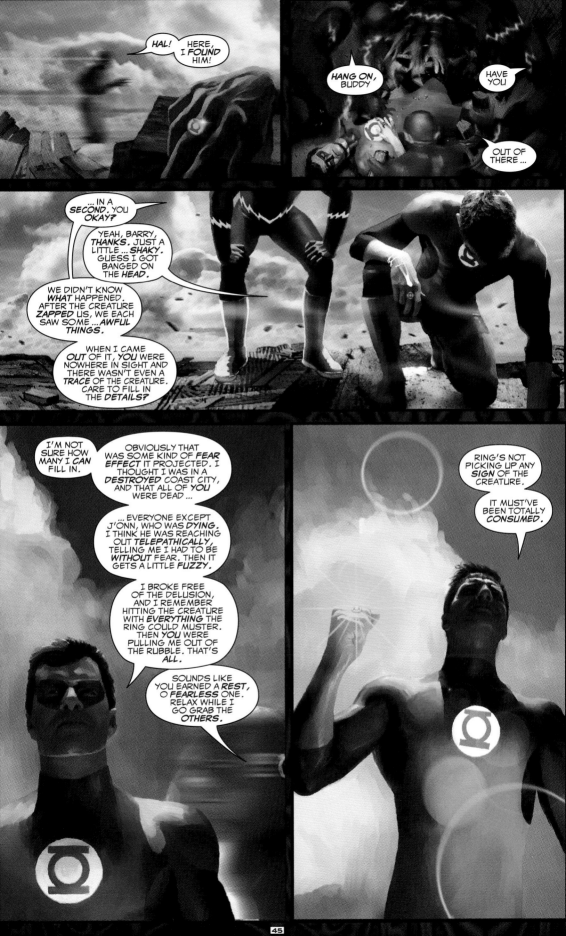

HAL! HERE, I **FOUND** HIM!

HANG ON, BUDDY

HAVE YOU

OUT OF THERE ...

... IN A **SECOND**. YOU **OKAY?**

YEAH, BARRY, **THANKS.** JUST A LITTLE ... **SHAKY.** GUESS I GOT BANGED ON THE **HEAD**.

WE DIDN'T KNOW **WHAT** HAPPENED. AFTER THE CREATURE **ZAPPED** US, WE EACH SAW SOME ... **AWFUL** THINGS.

WHEN I CAME **OUT** OF IT, **YOU** WERE NOWHERE IN SIGHT AND THERE WASN'T EVEN A **TRACE** OF THE CREATURE. CARE TO FILL IN THE **DETAILS?**

I'M NOT SURE HOW MANY I **CAN** FILL IN.

OBVIOUSLY THAT WAS SOME KIND OF **FEAR EFFECT** IT PROJECTED. I THOUGHT I WAS IN A **DESTROYED** COAST CITY, AND THAT ALL OF **YOU** WERE DEAD ...

... EVERYONE EXCEPT J'ONN, WHO WAS **DYING.** I THINK HE WAS REACHING OUT **TELEPATHICALLY,** TELLING ME I HAD TO BE **WITHOUT** FEAR. THEN IT GETS A LITTLE **FUZZY.**

I BROKE FREE OF THE DELUSION, AND I REMEMBER HITTING THE CREATURE WITH **EVERYTHING** THE RING COULD MUSTER. THEN **YOU** WERE PULLING ME OUT OF THE RUBBLE. THAT'S **ALL.**

SOUNDS LIKE YOU EARNED A **REST,** O **FEARLESS** ONE. RELAX WHILE I GO GRAB THE **OTHERS.**

RING'S NOT PICKING UP ANY **SIGN** OF THE CREATURE.

IT MUST'VE BEEN TOTALLY **CONSUMED.**

GOOD TO SEE EVERYTHING BACK IN ONE PIECE. MORE OR LESS, ANYWAY. WATCHING IT LAID WASTE ...
... THAT REALLY WAS THE MOST FRIGHTENING THING I'VE EVER EXPERIENCED.
I DON'T EVER WANT TO FACE SOMETHING LIKE THAT.
COME ON, HAL ...
... I DOUBT COAST CITY HAS MUCH TO WORRY ABOUT WITH YOU AROUND.
I HOPE YOU'RE RIGHT, DINAH.
OF COURSE SHE'S RIGHT, HAL. YOU KNOW BETTER THAN ANYONE ...
" ... THE GOOD GUYS ALWAYS WIN."

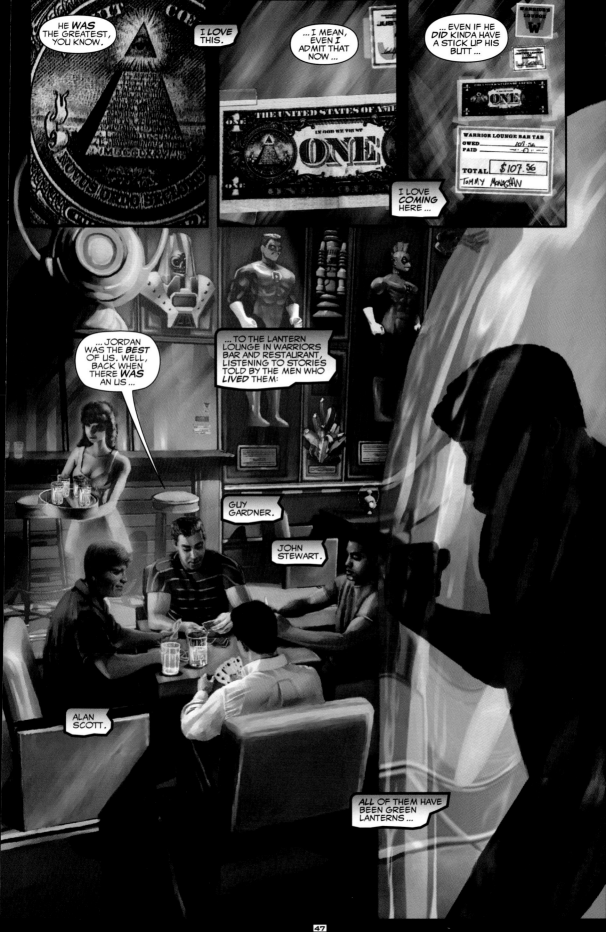

HE **WAS** THE GREATEST, YOU KNOW.

I LOVE THIS.

... I MEAN, EVEN **I** ADMIT THAT NOW ...

... EVEN IF HE **DID** KINDA HAVE A STICK UP HIS BUTT ...

WARRIOR LOUNGE BAR TAB
OWED _____ 107.56
PAID _____ -0-
TOTAL $107.56
TOMMY MONAGHAN

I LOVE COMING HERE ...

... JORDAN WAS THE **BEST** OF US. WELL, BACK WHEN THERE **WAS** AN US ...

... TO THE LANTERN LOUNGE IN WARRIORS BAR AND RESTAURANT, LISTENING TO STORIES TOLD BY THE MEN WHO **LIVED** THEM:

GUY GARDNER.

JOHN STEWART.

ALAN SCOTT.

ALL OF THEM HAVE BEEN GREEN LANTERNS ...

47

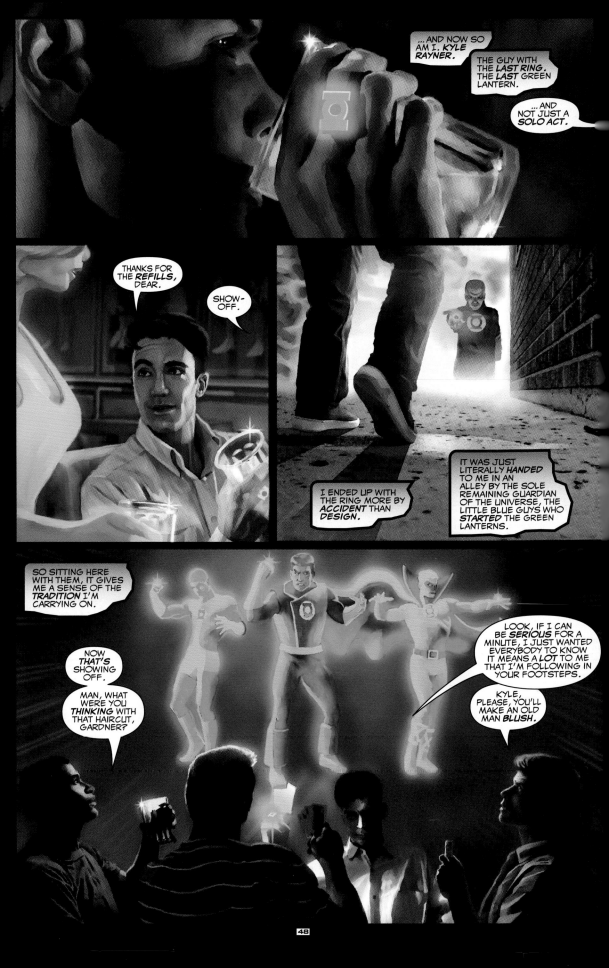

...AND NOW SO AM I. *KYLE RAYNER.*

THE GUY WITH THE *LAST RING.* THE *LAST* GREEN LANTERN.

...AND NOT JUST A *SOLO ACT.*

THANKS FOR THE *REFILLS,* DEAR.

SHOW-OFF.

I ENDED UP WITH THE RING MORE BY *ACCIDENT* THAN *DESIGN.*

IT WAS JUST LITERALLY *HANDED* TO ME IN AN ALLEY BY THE SOLE REMAINING GUARDIAN OF THE UNIVERSE, THE LITTLE BLUE GUYS WHO *STARTED* THE GREEN LANTERNS.

SO SITTING HERE WITH THEM, IT GIVES ME A SENSE OF THE *TRADITION* I'M CARRYING ON.

NOW *THAT'S* SHOWING OFF.

MAN, WHAT WERE YOU *THINKING* WITH THAT HAIRCUT, GARDNER?

LOOK, IF I CAN BE *SERIOUS* FOR A MINUTE, I JUST WANTED EVERYBODY TO KNOW IT MEANS A *LOT* TO ME THAT I'M FOLLOWING IN YOUR FOOTSTEPS.

KYLE, PLEASE, YOU'LL MAKE AN OLD MAN *BLUSH.*

NO, I'M SERIOUS ...
... ESPECIALLY YOU, GUY. YOU'RE MY ROLE MODEL.
LADIES AND GENTLEMEN, THE SOUNDS OF SARCASM.
ALL RIGHT, ALL RIGHT, YOU COME HERE TO PLAY CARDS OR MAKE FUN OF THE PROPRIETOR? LAST HAND ...
... FIVE-CARD DRAW, NO WILD CARDS.
I'LL TELL YOU, KID, YOU GOT IT EASY PLAYING HERO NOW.
EASY? ACCORDING TO WHO, GUY?
I'M JUST SAYING IT'S EASIER NOW THAN WHEN WE WERE IN THE TRENCHES.
SEE, ALAN FOR INSTANCE, WHEN HE WAS GREEN LANTERN YOU HAD THE NAZIS. BIG WORLDWIDE THREAT, RIGHT?
AND WHEN JOHN AND I WERE SUITED UP, YOU HAD THE COMMIES. COLD WAR, BIG RED MACHINE TRYING TO TAKE OVER THE PLANET.
I THINK YOU WERE MORE WORRIED ABOUT THEM THAN I WAS.
NOT THE POINT. WHAT I'M SAYING IS, THERE WAS ALWAYS AN ENEMY. A BIG THEM AGAINST US. BUT NOW ...
... NOW THERE'S NO THEM. JUST YOUR USUAL MIXED NUTS EVERY HERO GETS HIT WITH.
YEAH, I SUPPOSE IT IS A DIFFERENT WORLD WITH NO OVERALL BOOGEYMAN. MAYBE THAT'S WHY EVERYBODY'S SO CAUGHT UP IN THEIR OWN LIVES ...
... SOUL-SEARCHING, SELF-DOUBTING, THAT WHOLE THING. EVERYBODY'S BUSY FIGHTING INDIVIDUAL BATTLES TO KEEP THEIR OWN LITTLE CORNER OF THE WORLD IN ONE PIECE.

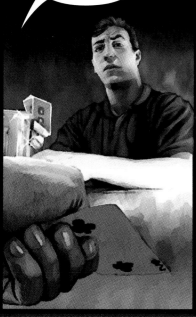

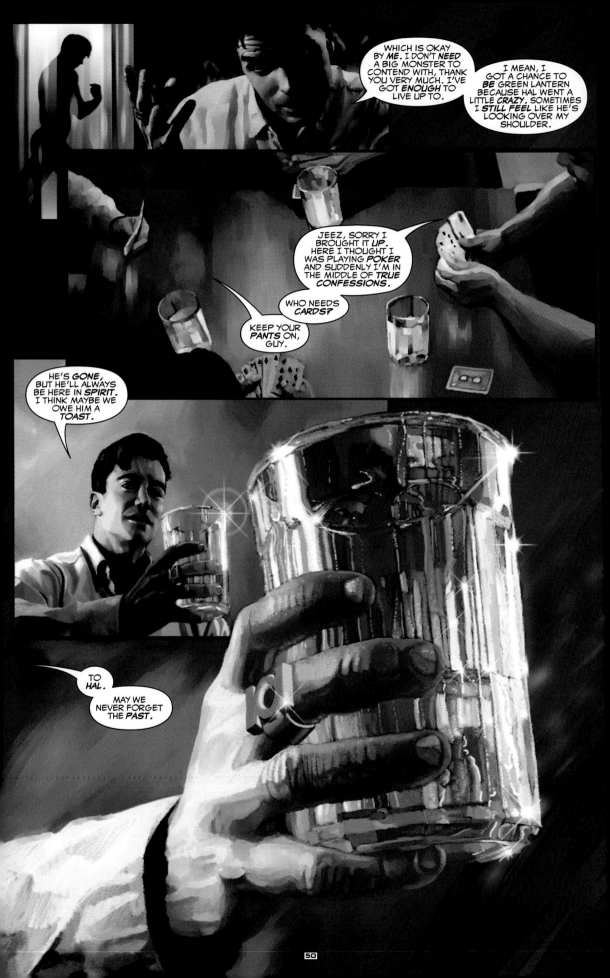

WHICH IS OKAY BY *ME.* I DON'T *NEED* A BIG MONSTER TO CONTEND WITH, THANK YOU VERY MUCH. I'VE GOT *ENOUGH* TO LIVE UP TO.

I MEAN, I GOT A CHANCE TO *BE* GREEN LANTERN BECAUSE HAL WENT A LITTLE *CRAZY.* SOMETIMES I *STILL FEEL* LIKE HE'S LOOKING OVER MY SHOULDER.

JEEZ, SORRY I BROUGHT IT *UP.* HERE I THOUGHT I WAS PLAYING *POKER* AND SUDDENLY I'M IN THE MIDDLE OF *TRUE CONFESSIONS.*

WHO NEEDS *CARDS?*

KEEP YOUR *PANTS* ON, GUY.

HE'S *GONE,* BUT HE'LL ALWAYS BE HERE IN *SPIRIT.* I THINK MAYBE WE OWE HIM A *TOAST.*

TO *HAL.*

MAY WE NEVER FORGET THE *PAST.*

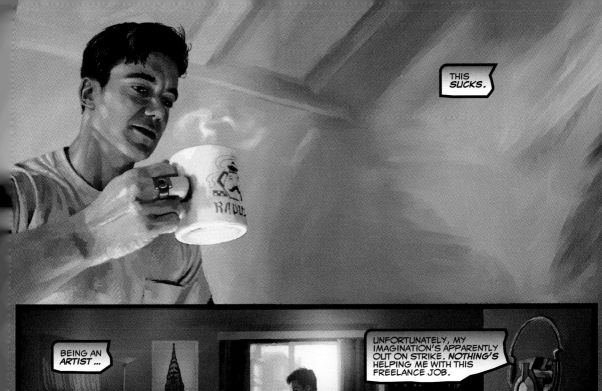

THIS *SUCKS.*

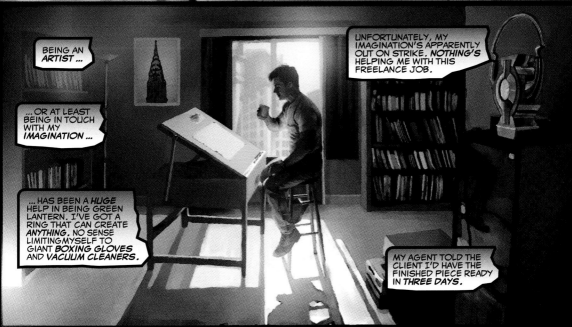

BEING AN *ARTIST* ...

... OR AT LEAST BEING IN TOUCH WITH MY *IMAGINATION* ...

... HAS BEEN A *HUGE* HELP IN BEING GREEN LANTERN. I'VE GOT A RING THAT CAN CREATE *ANYTHING.* NO SENSE LIMITING MYSELF TO GIANT *BOXING GLOVES* AND *VACUUM CLEANERS.*

UNFORTUNATELY, MY IMAGINATION'S APPARENTLY OUT ON STRIKE. *NOTHING'S* HELPING ME WITH THIS FREELANCE JOB.

MY AGENT TOLD THE CLIENT I'D HAVE THE FINISHED PIECE READY IN *THREE DAYS.*

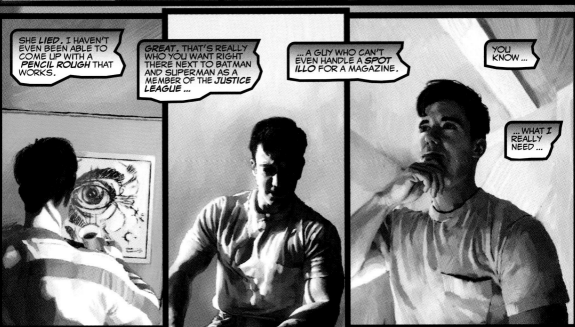

SHE *LIED.* I HAVEN'T EVEN BEEN ABLE TO COME UP WITH A *PENCIL ROUGH* THAT WORKS.

GREAT. THAT'S REALLY WHO YOU WANT RIGHT THERE NEXT TO BATMAN AND SUPERMAN AS A MEMBER OF THE *JUSTICE LEAGUE* ...

... A GUY WHO CAN'T EVEN HANDLE A *SPOT ILLO* FOR A MAGAZINE.

YOU KNOW ...

... WHAT *I* REALLY NEED ...

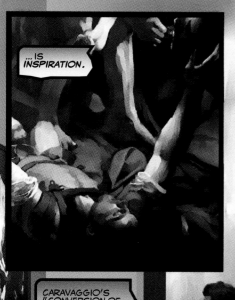

... IS *INSPIRATION*.

THIS IS MY *FAVORITE* PLACE ON THE PLANET. ON *ANY* PLANET.

CARAVAGGIO'S *"CONVERSION OF ST. PAUL."* A YOUNG WARRIOR KNOCKED FROM HIS HORSE IN A RAY OF *ENLIGHTENMENT*.

AS MANY TIMES AS I'VE *STUDIED* IT, IT'S STILL *BEYOND* ME. I SUPPOSE THAT'S WHAT SEPARATES *MASTERPIECES* FROM ELVIS AT THE LAST SUPPER ON BLACK VELVET.

I'M *LUCKY* TO BE LIVING IN NEW YORK, ONE OF THE WORLD'S *GREAT* ART MUSEUMS IS A SUBWAY AWAY. WHENEVER I'M FEELING *EMPTY* ...

... I COME TO THE MET AND *SURROUND* MYSELF WITH THE ART-WORK, EVEN *COPY* A PAINTING TO UNDERSTAND THE TECHNIQUE.

THIS IS HOW *I* GET RECHARGED.

... *GATHER* IN WORSHIP ...

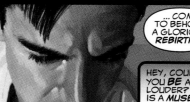

... *COME* TO BEHOLD A GLORIOUS *REBIRTH* ...

HEY, COULD YOU *BE* ANY LOUDER? THIS IS A *MUSEUM*.

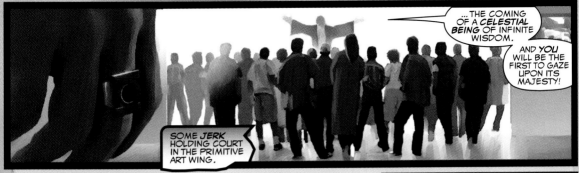

... THE COMING OF A *CELESTIAL BEING* OF INFINITE WISDOM.

AND *YOU* WILL BE THE FIRST TO GAZE UPON ITS MAJESTY!

SOME *JERK* HOLDING COURT IN THE PRIMITIVE ART WING.

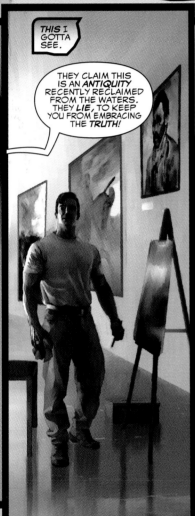

THIS I GOTTA SEE.

THEY CLAIM THIS IS AN *ANTIQUITY* RECENTLY RECLAIMED FROM THE WATERS. THEY *LIE*, TO KEEP YOU FROM EMBRACING THE *TRUTH!*

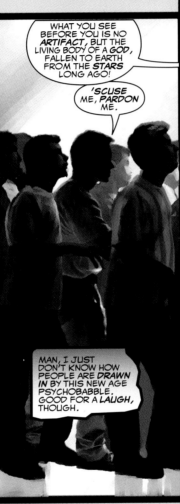

WHAT YOU SEE BEFORE YOU IS NO *ARTIFACT*, BUT THE LIVING BODY OF A *GOD*, FALLEN TO EARTH FROM THE *STARS* LONG AGO!

'SCUSE ME, *PARDON* ME.

MAN, I JUST DON'T KNOW HOW PEOPLE ARE *DRAWN IN* BY THIS NEW AGE PSYCHOBABBLE. GOOD FOR A *LAUGH*, THOUGH.

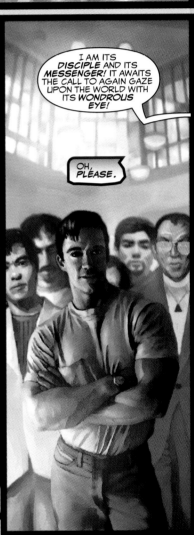

I AM ITS *DISCIPLE* AND ITS *MESSENGER!* IT AWAITS THE CALL TO AGAIN GAZE UPON THE WORLD WITH ITS *WONDROUS EYE!*

OH, *PLEASE.*

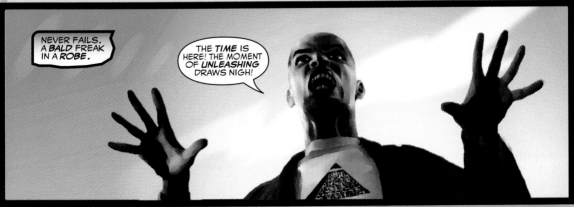

NEVER FAILS. A *BALD* FREAK IN A *ROBE.*

THE *TIME* IS HERE! THE MOMENT OF *UNLEASHING* DRAWS NIGH!

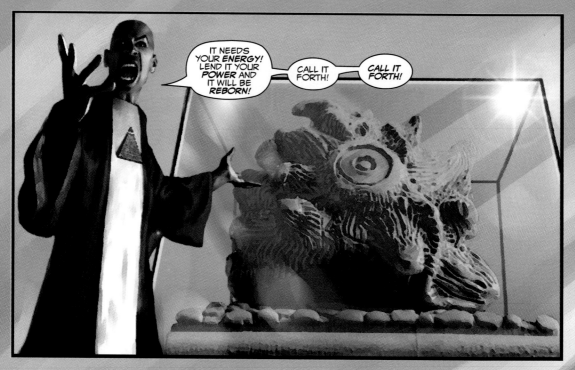

IT NEEDS YOUR ENERGY! LEND IT YOUR POWER AND IT WILL BE REBORN!

CALL IT FORTH!

CALL IT FORTH!

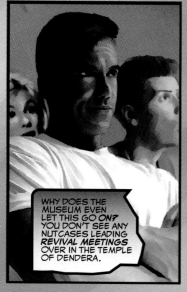

WHY DOES THE MUSEUM EVEN LET THIS GO ON? YOU DON'T SEE ANY NUTCASES LEADING REVIVAL MEETINGS OVER IN THE TEMPLE OF DENDERA.

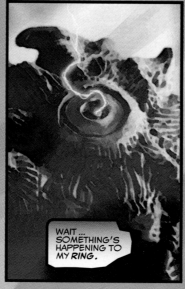

WAIT ... SOMETHING'S HAPPENING TO MY RING.

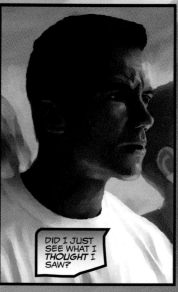

DID I JUST SEE WHAT I THOUGHT I SAW?

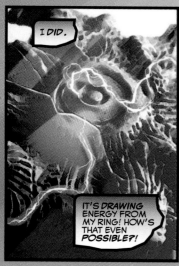

I DID.

IT'S DRAWING ENERGY FROM MY RING! HOW'S THAT EVEN POSSIBLE?!

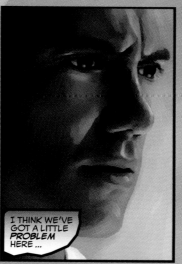

I THINK WE'VE GOT A LITTLE PROBLEM HERE ...

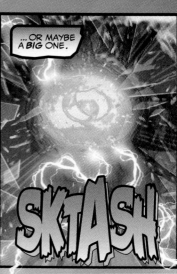

... OR MAYBE A BIG ONE.

SKTASH

HE'S LATE.
5:18
THIS MEETING OF THE JUSTICE LEAGUE WAS TO HAVE STARTED EIGHTEEN MINUTES AGO, AND GREEN LANTERN STILL HASN'T ARRIVED.
I'M NOT TERRIBLY PLEASED ABOUT COMING ALL THE WAY TO THE MOON TO BE HERE AT THE WATCHTOWER, MUCH LESS HAVING MY TIME WASTED.
IS ANYBODY REALLY SURPRISED THE POSTER CHILD FOR THE PUNCTUALLY HANDICAPPED DIDN'T MAKE IT AGAIN?
ANYBODY?
SHOW OF HANDS?
THIS IS KYLE WE'RE TALKING ABOUT. HE'S PROBABLY OFF FOOLING AROUND SOMEWHERE AND FORGOT WHEN THE MEETING--
BREEPBREEPBREEP
WHAT? WHAT'S GOING ON?

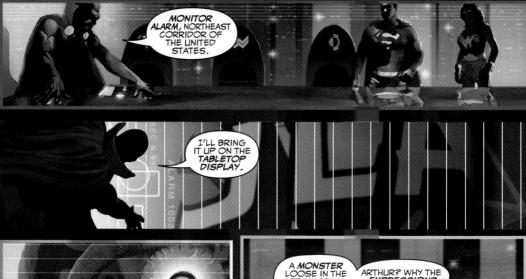

MONITOR ALARM, NORTHEAST CORRIDOR OF THE UNITED STATES.

I'LL BRING IT UP ON THE TABLETOP DISPLAY.

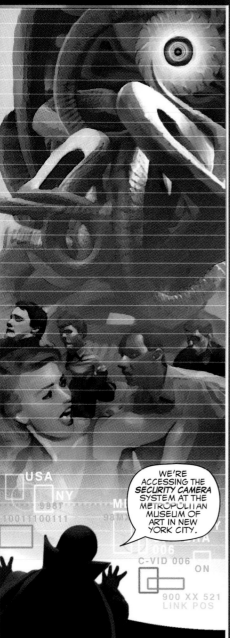

WE'RE ACCESSING THE SECURITY CAMERA SYSTEM AT THE METROPOLITAN MUSEUM OF ART IN NEW YORK CITY.

USA
NY

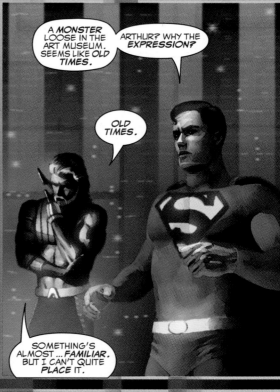

A MONSTER LOOSE IN THE ART MUSEUM. SEEMS LIKE OLD TIMES.

ARTHUR? WHY THE EXPRESSION?

OLD TIMES.

SOMETHING'S ALMOST ...FAMILIAR. BUT I CAN'T QUITE PLACE IT.

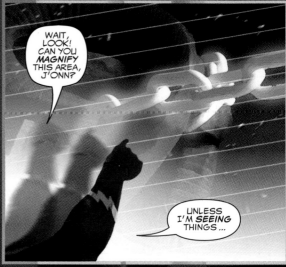

WAIT, LOOK! CAN YOU MAGNIFY THIS AREA, J'ONN?

UNLESS I'M SEEING THINGS ...

"...WE JUST *FOUND* OUR BOY."

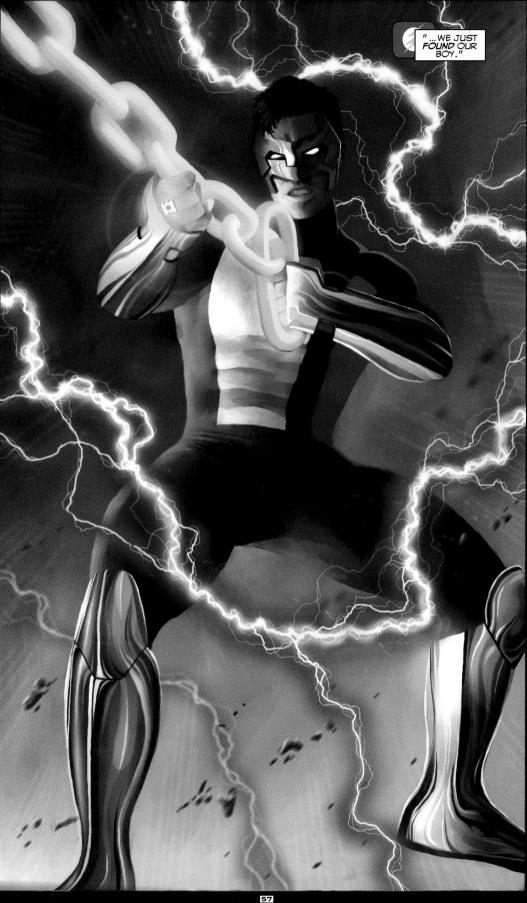

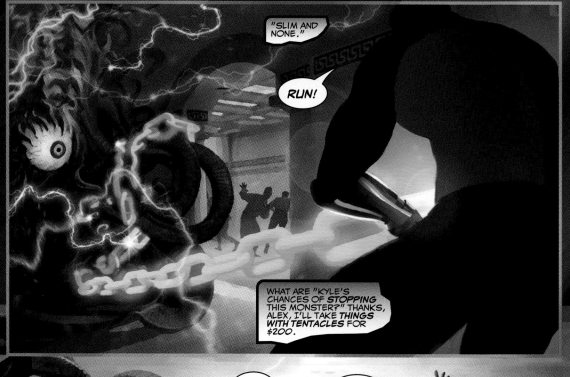

"SLIM AND NONE."

RUN!

WHAT ARE "KYLE'S CHANCES OF *STOPPING* THIS MONSTER?" THANKS, ALEX, I'LL TAKE *THINGS WITH TENTACLES* FOR $200.

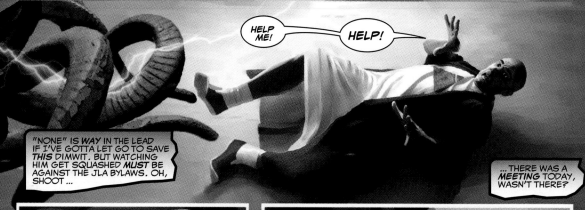

HELP ME!

HELP!

"NONE" IS *WAY* IN THE LEAD IF I'VE GOTTA LET GO TO SAVE *THIS* DIMWIT. BUT WATCHING HIM GET SQUASHED *MUST* BE AGAINST THE JLA BYLAWS. OH, SHOOT ...

... THERE WAS A *MEETING* TODAY, WASN'T THERE?

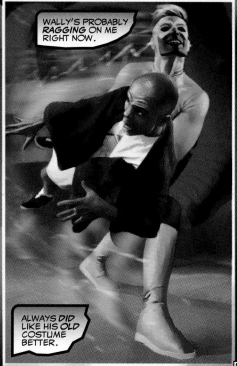

WALLY'S PROBABLY *RAGGING* ON ME RIGHT NOW.

ALWAYS *DID* LIKE HIS *OLD* COSTUME BETTER.

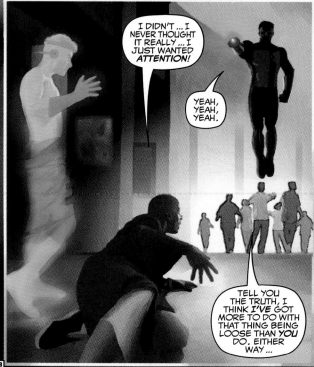

I DIDN'T ... I NEVER THOUGHT IT REALLY ... I JUST WANTED *ATTENTION!*

YEAH, YEAH, YEAH.

TELL YOU THE TRUTH, I THINK I'VE GOT MORE TO DO WITH THAT THING BEING LOOSE THAN *YOU* DO. EITHER WAY ...

"...I'M THE STOOGE WHO GETS TO CLEAN UP AFTER IT."
WHAT AM I SUPPOSED TO DO? THE BEAST FROM 20,000 FATHOMS HERE KEEPS GROWING LIKE JACK'S BEANSTALK ...
...AND IT JUST ABSORBS WHATEVER RING CREATION I THROW AT IT. BUT IF I STAND BY AND DO NOTHING ...
...WELL, I CAN'T STAND BY AND DO NOTHING. I SO DON'T LIKE WHERE THIS WHOLE THING IS GO--
THWUMP
--NNG!

I KNOW THIS THING.
IT'S DIFFERENT, IT'S GROWN, BUT I'M CERTAIN IT'S THE SAME CREATURE.
FROM COAST CITY. THAT'S IT, ISN'T IT?
SO HAL DIDN'T KILL IT. HE JUST... STOPPED IT. MAYBE IT WENT INTO A DORMANT STATE.
THIS IS SOMETHING WE FACED BEFORE, WHEN THE JUSTICE LEAGUE FIRST GOT TOGETHER. HAL JORDAN WAS RESPONSIBLE FOR DEFEATING IT.
BARRY NEVER MENTIONED IT TO ME.
IT WAS BEATEN BEFORE; WE'LL FIND A WAY TO DO IT AGAIN.
HEAD FOR THE TRANSPORTERS; WE'LL GIVE KYLE A HAND.
I DUNNO, MAYBE WE SHOULD LET HIM GET OUTTA THIS ONE HIMSELF.
WALLY.
KIDDING, OKAY? I WAS JUST--
WHAT HAPPENED?
POWER FAILURE.

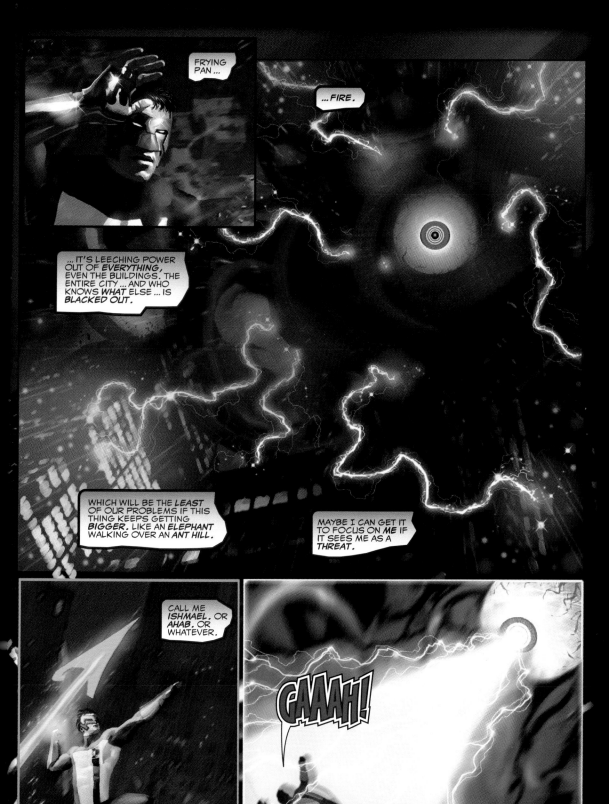

FRYING PAN...

...FIRE.

... IT'S LEECHING POWER OUT OF *EVERYTHING*, EVEN THE BUILDINGS. THE ENTIRE CITY ... AND WHO KNOWS *WHAT* ELSE ... IS *BLACKED OUT*.

WHICH WILL BE THE *LEAST* OF OUR PROBLEMS IF THIS THING KEEPS GETTING *BIGGER*. LIKE AN *ELEPHANT* WALKING OVER AN *ANT HILL*.

MAYBE I CAN GET IT TO FOCUS ON *ME* IF IT SEES ME AS A *THREAT*.

CALL ME *ISHMAEL*. OR *AHAB*. OR WHATEVER.

GAAAH!

LOOK OVER *HERE*, YOU UG--

THE JLA LAUGHING AT ME
FAILURE
WHAT MAJOR FORCE DID TO ALEX
FAILURE
DONNA WALKING AWAY FROM ME
FAILURE
PARALLAX UNLEASHED
FAILURE
NOT WORTHY OF GANTHET'S GIFT
FAILURE

FAILURE ...
... FAILURE ...
... UFF!
I HADN'T LEFT TOWN YET. LUCKILY. ARE YOU ALL RIGHT?
ALAN? WHAT ARE YOU--
YEAH ...

... YEAH, I GUESS SO. I DON'T KNOW *WHAT* IT HIT ME WITH. IT WAS LIKE ...
... *IMAGES* IN MY HEAD. STUFF STRAIGHT FROM MY *NIGHTMARES*. LIKE BEING CONFRONTED WITH--
YOUR *FEARS?*
YEAH. HOW DID *YOU* KNOW?
I *FOUGHT* THIS CREATURE YEARS AGO. I THOUGHT I DESTROYED IT *THEN*. APPARENTLY I WAS *WRONG*.
THAT THING IT DOES IS SOME SORT OF *FEAR-INDUCING* DEFENSE MECHANISM. IT FORCED *ME* TO FACE A WORLD WHERE THE THIRD REICH WAS *VICTORIOUS*.
IT SHOWED *YOU* WHAT YOU WERE AFRAID OF, IT SHOWED *ME* THE SAME THING. BUT MINE WAS STRICTLY *PERSONAL*.
REMEMBER WHAT WE WERE TALKING ABOUT AT *WARRIORS?* MAYBE THAT'S WHY IT JUST STAYED WITH ME BRIEFLY ...
... BECAUSE THE FEARS WERE *MINE ALONE*.
BUT THE ENTIRE WORLD REALLY *IS* AT RISK. WHAT'S TO STOP THE CREATURE FROM DRAINING POWER *WORLDWIDE?*
WHO KNOWS *WHAT* WE'D BE FACING THEN. WE NEED TO *ACT*, KYLE.
THEN WHY ARE WE HANGING AROUND *TALKING* ...
... LET'S GO *GET* IT.
KYLE! *WAIT!*
KIDS TODAY.

RING'S GOT A PRETTY FULL CHARGE. YOU WANT ENERGY?
LET'S FIND OUT HOW MUCH IS TOO MUCH.
HEY!
ALAN, WHAT'D YOU DO THAT FOR?!
BECAUSE PUMPING THAT THING FULL OF ENERGY IS THE LAST THING YOU WANT TO DO. IN FACT ...
... IT MIGHT BE THE LAST THING YOU DO.
IT'S WHAT I DID WHEN I FOUGHT IT.
AND LOOK AT IT NOW. IT'S COME BACK BIGGER AND MORE POWERFUL.
WE CAN'T RISK THAT HAPPENING AGAIN, KYLE. WE HAVE TO PUT AN END TO IT.
WELL, IF YOU HAVE ANY SUGGESTIONS ...
... NOW WOULD BE THE TIME.

"THERE'S ONLY ONE OPTION ..."
...WE HAVE TO FIND A WAY TO STOP IT PERMANENTLY.
ALAN, IT'S THE SIZE OF STATEN ISLAND.
SEEMS LIKE ALL IT WANTS IS ENERGY. MAYBE IF WE LET IT HAVE IT ...
KYLE ...
" ...WE'RE NOT RISKING THE END OF THE WORLD ON A GUESS! NO, THIS WAY IS--"
--AAAH!
SHRAKOOM
ALAN!

EASY, ALAN. I GOTCHA.
THANKS FOR THE ...
... THE CATCH ...
I OWED YOU ONE.
RELAX. YOU'LL BE OKAY.
NONE OF US ... ARE GOING TO BE OKAY. I DON'T MATTER, KYLE ... YOU DON'T MATTER ...
... ONLY STOPPING THAT THING.
ALAN, THE CREATURE HASN'T ATTACKED UNLESS IT'S BEEN PROVOKED, RIGHT?
I STILL THINK OUR BEST SHOT MIGHT BE TO LET IT DO WHAT IT'S TRYING TO DO ...
... MAYBE EVEN HELP IT.
YOU CAN'T TAKE THAT CHANCE. THERE'S NO OTHER WAY ...
... YOU HAVE TO KILL IT.
IT'S UP TO YOU TO FINISH THIS, KYLE.
ALL RIGHT ...

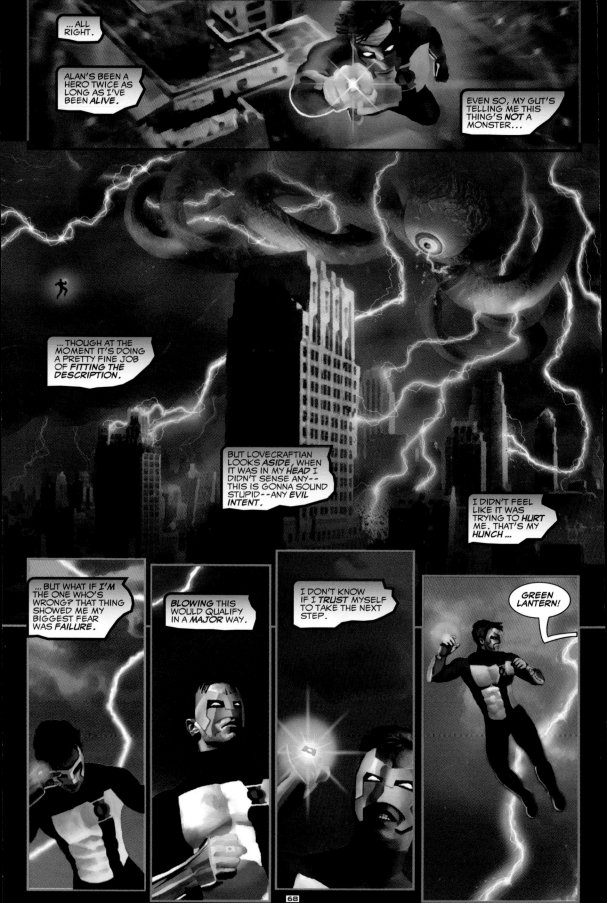

... ALL RIGHT.

ALAN'S BEEN A HERO TWICE AS LONG AS I'VE BEEN *ALIVE*.

EVEN SO, MY GUT'S TELLING ME THIS THING'S *NOT* A MONSTER...

... THOUGH AT THE MOMENT IT'S DOING A PRETTY FINE JOB OF *FITTING THE DESCRIPTION*.

BUT LOVECRAFTIAN LOOKS *ASIDE*, WHEN IT WAS IN MY *HEAD* I DIDN'T SENSE ANY-- THIS IS GONNA SOUND STUPID--ANY *EVIL INTENT*.

I DIDN'T FEEL LIKE IT WAS TRYING TO *HURT* ME. THAT'S MY HUNCH ...

... BUT WHAT IF *I'M* THE ONE WHO'S WRONG? THAT THING SHOWED ME MY BIGGEST FEAR WAS *FAILURE*.

BLOWING THIS WOULD QUALIFY IN A *MAJOR* WAY.

I DON'T KNOW IF I *TRUST* MYSELF TO TAKE THE NEXT STEP.

GREEN LANTERN!

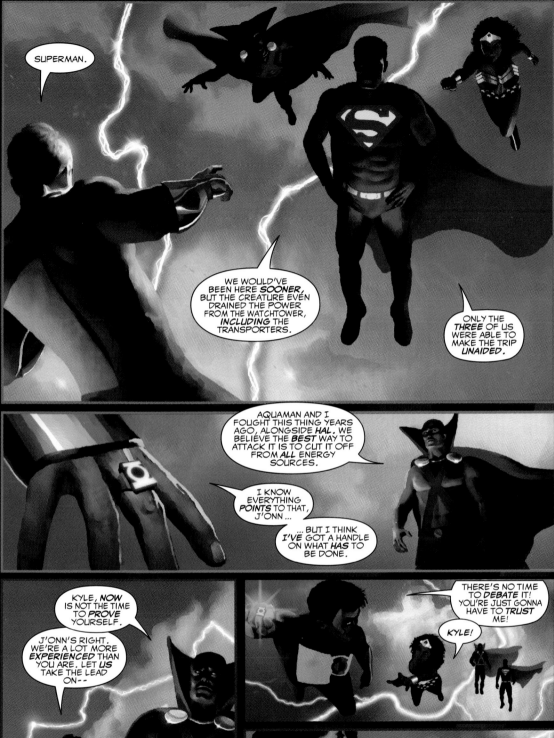

SUPERMAN.

WE WOULD'VE BEEN HERE *SOONER*, BUT THE CREATURE EVEN DRAINED THE POWER FROM THE WATCHTOWER, *INCLUDING THE TRANSPORTERS.*

ONLY THE *THREE* OF US WERE ABLE TO MAKE THE TRIP *UNAIDED.*

AQUAMAN AND I FOUGHT THIS THING YEARS AGO, ALONGSIDE *HAL.* WE BELIEVE THE *BEST* WAY TO ATTACK IT IS TO CUT IT OFF FROM *ALL* ENERGY SOURCES.

I KNOW EVERYTHING *POINTS* TO THAT, *J'ONN* ...

... BUT I THINK *I'VE* GOT A HANDLE ON WHAT *HAS* TO BE DONE.

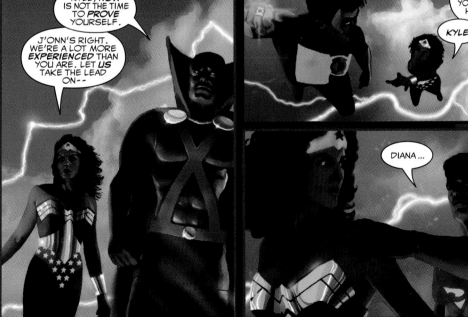

KYLE, *NOW* IS NOT THE TIME TO *PROVE* YOURSELF.

J'ONN'S RIGHT. WE'RE A LOT MORE *EXPERIENCED* THAN YOU ARE. LET *US* TAKE THE LEAD ON--

THERE'S NO TIME TO *DEBATE* IT! YOU'RE JUST GONNA HAVE TO *TRUST* ME!

KYLE!

DIANA ...

... HE'S EARNED AT LEAST *THAT* MUCH.

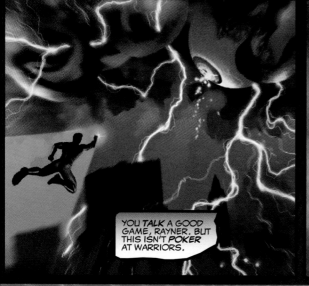

YOU *TALK* A GOOD GAME, RAYNER. BUT THIS ISN'T *POKER* AT WARRIORS.

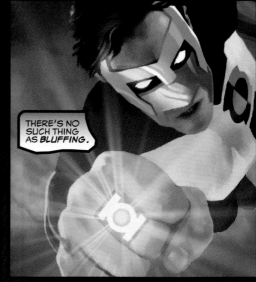

THERE'S NO SUCH THING AS *BLUFFING.*

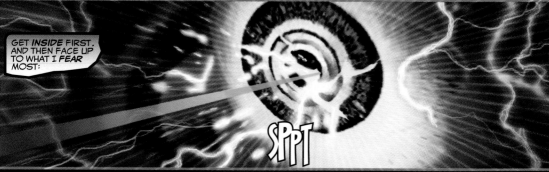

GET *INSIDE* FIRST. AND THEN FACE UP TO WHAT I *FEAR* MOST:

SPPT

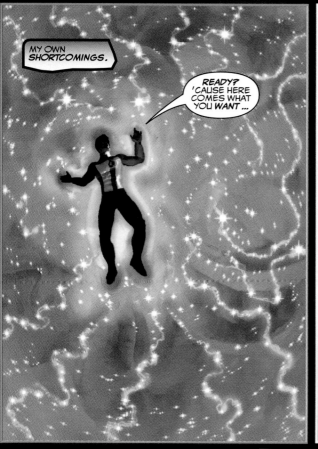

MY OWN *SHORTCOMINGS.*

READY? 'CAUSE HERE COMES WHAT YOU *WANT* ...

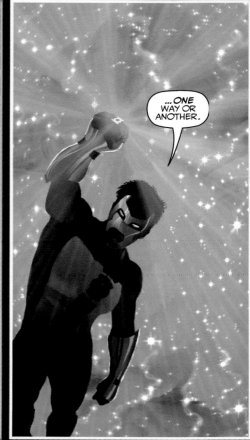

...ONE WAY OR ANOTHER.

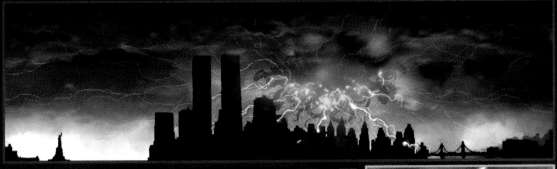

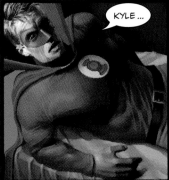

KYLE...

HE'S *INSIDE* THE THING?

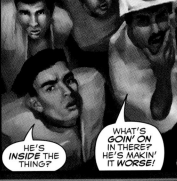

WHAT'S *GOIN'* ON IN THERE? HE'S MAKIN' IT *WORSE!*

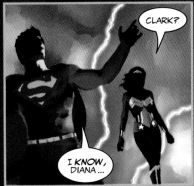

CLARK?

I *KNOW*, DIANA...

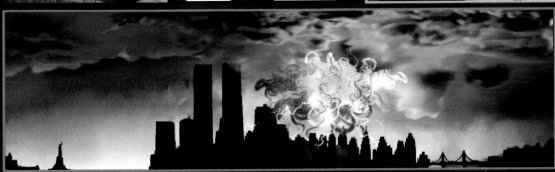

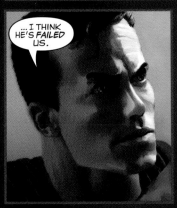

...I THINK HE'S *FAILED* US.

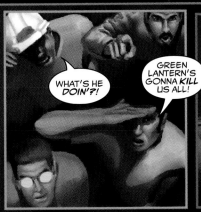

WHAT'S HE *DOIN'?!*

GREEN LANTERN'S GONNA *KILL* US ALL!

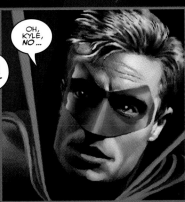

OH, KYLE, NO...

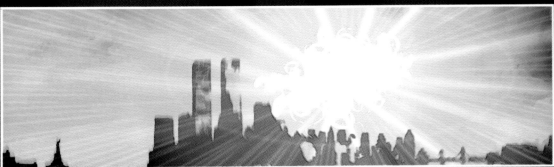

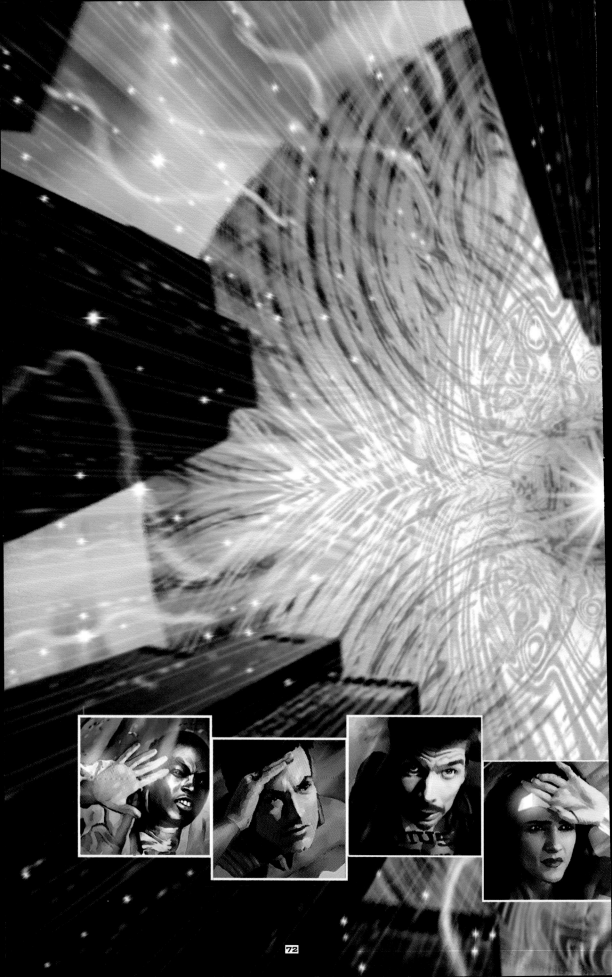

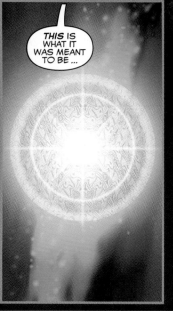

THIS IS WHAT IT WAS MEANT TO BE...

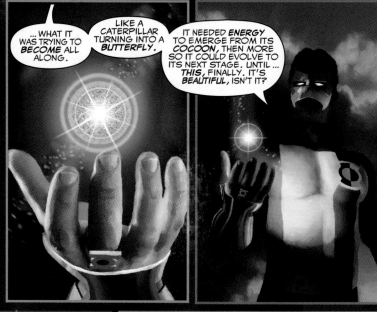

...WHAT IT WAS TRYING TO *BECOME* ALL ALONG.

LIKE A CATERPILLAR TURNING INTO A *BUTTERFLY.*

IT NEEDED *ENERGY* TO EMERGE FROM ITS *COCOON,* THEN MORE SO IT COULD EVOLVE TO ITS NEXT STAGE, UNTIL... *THIS,* FINALLY. IT'S *BEAUTIFUL,* ISN'T IT?

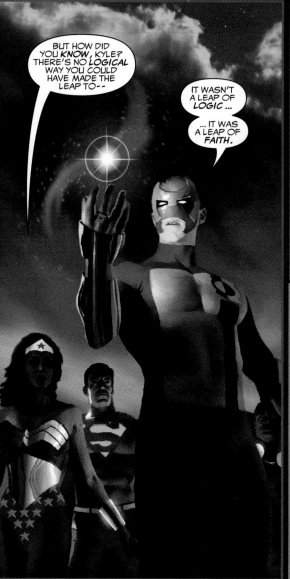

BUT HOW DID YOU *KNOW,* KYLE? THERE'S NO *LOGICAL* WAY YOU COULD HAVE MADE THE LEAP TO--

IT WASN'T A LEAP OF *LOGIC*...

...IT WAS A LEAP OF *FAITH.*

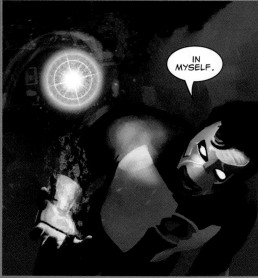

IN MYSELF.

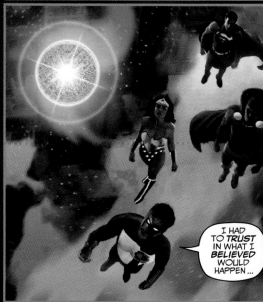

I HAD TO *TRUST* IN WHAT I *BELIEVED* WOULD HAPPEN...

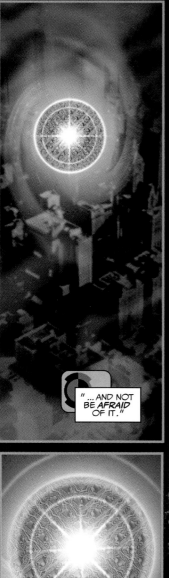

" ...AND NOT BE *AFRAID* OF IT."

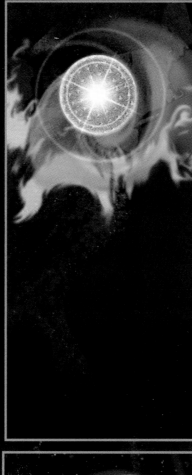

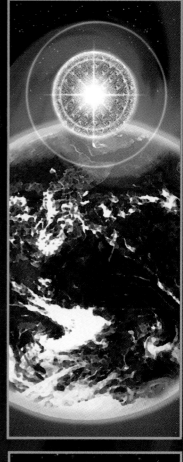

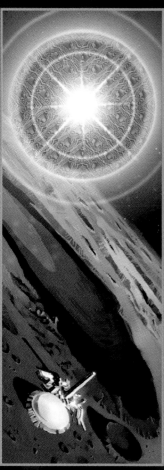

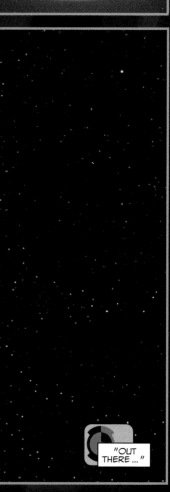

"OUT THERE ..."

... SOMEWHERE.
IT'S OUT THERE SOMEWHERE DOING ... WELL, I CAN'T EVEN GUESS AT THAT. I'D LOVE TO KNOW WHAT BECAME OF IT.
AS FAR AS THAT GOES, I'D LOVE TO KNOW WHAT IT WAS IN THE FIRST PLACE.
WHAT DO YOU THINK?
WHAT I THINK IS THERE'S MORE IN THE WIDE UNIVERSE THAN WE'LL EVER KNOW. WHATEVER IT WAS, IT CAME TO EARTH FROM THE STARS A LONG TIME AGO ...
... AND IT WAITED FOR THE POWER TO SET IT FREE SO IT COULD EVENTUALLY RETURN TO THE STARS. IT'S A LIFEFORM BEYOND OUR UNDERSTANDING, KYLE.
BUT YOU WERE THE ONLY ONE WHO DIDN'T SEE IT AS A MONSTER. YOU WEREN'T SCARED.
YES I WAS SCARED. I JUST MANAGED TO OVERCOME MY OWN FEARS.
WHAT'S THAT THING SOME PRESIDENT SAID? THE ONLY THING YOU HAVE TO FEAR IS FEAR ITSELF.
SOUNDS RIGHT TO ME ...

...'CAUSE I'VE ONLY HEARD OF ONE GUY WHO WAS FEARLESS.
THE END

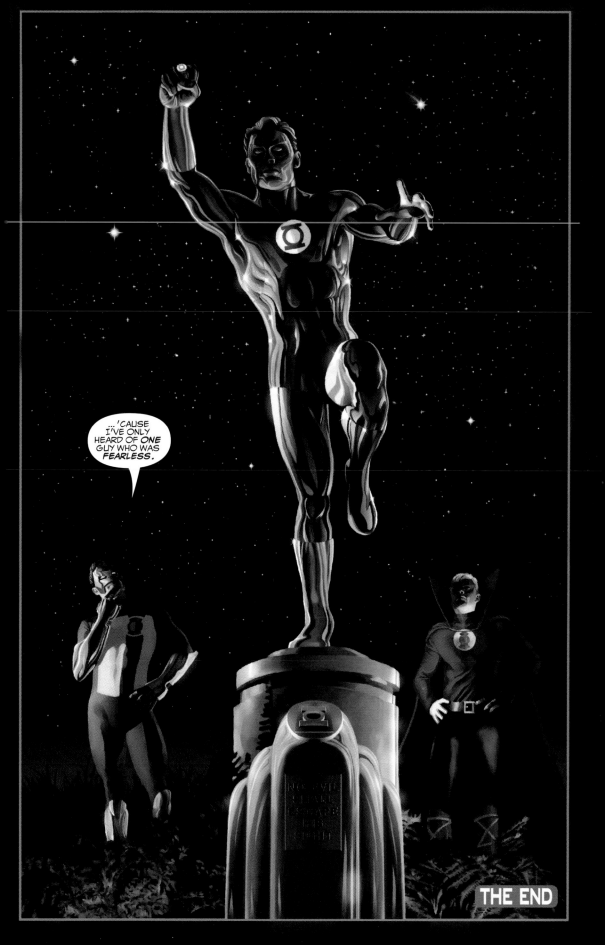

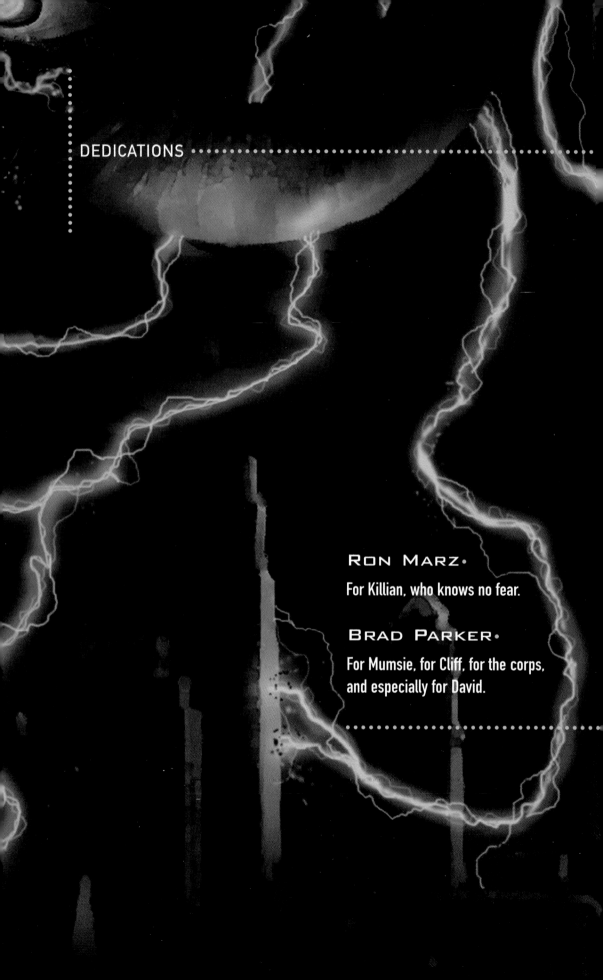

DEDICATIONS

RON MARZ·

For Killian, who knows no fear.

BRAD PARKER·

For Mumsie, for Cliff, for the corps,
and especially for David.